MURDER IN THE FOREST LAB

Utterly Addictive Cozy Mystery

Carolina Cozy Mysteries

ANDREA KRESS

Andrea Kress 2023

Chapter 1

The day was cold, and the sky was clear as Gemma drove south from D. C. It had been wise to spend the night before at her sister's place in Philadelphia rather than start out from her home in New Jersey, not only because it shaved some hours off the trip, but the worst of the traffic was behind her. She had already faced the capital's almost bumper-to-bumper Beltway traffic, and now she was on a long stretch with nothing to see on the side of the road but trees.

The spark of excitement was still with her—and mercifully not a shred of anxiety —as she had left a marriage, an apartment and the toxic job in Manhattan's most vicious industry: advertising. During COVID the staff had been forced to work from home and that turned out to be a double-edged sword. It was a blessing not to have to get dressed up, deal with her hair and makeup, take the crowded subway from Brooklyn to Manhattan only to face her odious boss. Suddenly, everyone worked from home and meetings were on Zoom, where only your torso was visible. She missed some of her co-workers but relished working in a quiet environment without the stress of her supervisor suddenly appearing at the side of her cubicle staring at her computer screen.

But working from home meant her husband was doing the same, and what small cracks existed in their relationship were rent wide with the monotony of their lives in isolation. She finished her work in record time each day just to get out of the apartment and walk. It didn't matter where she went, or how bad the weather was, it was getting out of that stifling atmosphere that got her through another day.

By the following summer the renewal on the apartment's lease had come due and she told Phil rather bluntly that she didn't want to live there anymore. She was going to move back to her father's house in New Jersey and work remotely from there as the world opened up. Not surprisingly, he took the announcement without emotion, which made her think that he didn't understand the full import of what she was proposing.

"Divorce," she added.

"Yes, I figured. It's sort of run its course."

That's all he said before putting headphones on and returning to his own workstation on the other side of the tiny living room.

The following year she lived in her father's house. He was glad of the company, and she relished the suburban quiet, not once missing the constant noise of the City and the crush of people. Foremost in her mind was when she might be required to return to work in person or whether the company would maintain the remote work. It had been a low stress year, but it was time to look for a new job. Something related to marketing but different. And for the first time, she let herself think outside of the New York City box that she had put herself in. She could go anywhere. With that expanded mindset she came upon an ad for a communications director at the Colter Primate Center in Leesborough, North Carolina.

What? Where? A Google search showed a modern building in what appeared to be a wooded area. That could mean a nice view out a window instead of the back of someone else's cubicle. It seemed to be physically located in a small town but was part of the larger Raleigh area, and she scrolled and clicked and liked what she saw. The cost of living was lower than the greater New York area—but what wasn't? The remuneration was listed as DOE, depending upon experience, and might be lower than what she was used to, but those two factors could balance out. From what she read, it appeared that she would be the only employee doing the communications job, probably liaising with the media and the nearby university with which the center was affiliated. That was a bonus. No more jockeying for the plum assignments, mentally elbowing fellow employees out of the way, keeping her head down in tumultuous times of listening to her boss's rambling diatribes about the team's not coming up with fresh ideas.

Gemma's mind was filled with bucolic images and smiling faces of innocuous academic types who likely had no concept of marketing. She went for a walk and let the pleasant thoughts develop into a universe entirely unlike the one she had known in the City, and by the time her three miles were accomplished, she was online again looking up information on the director of the Colter Center. World renowned in his field, recipient of many grants and awards and, according to the photo, a dapper, middle-aged man who looked to have a decisive demeanor. She drafted a response to the advertisement, attaching her resume, and hit *send* with the excitement one only feels when trying something new.

To her surprise, he responded within the hour and suggested a Zoom call the next day at eight a.m. Gemma's stomach clenched at the thought of having to fish out her makeup bag from some drawer, get her hair in order and determine what best to wear. Nothing too artsy, probably a blouse and blazer.

The interview couldn't have gone better, and Doctor Werner was charm itself. Erudite, as she expected, but also charming, and he explicitly said he was looking for someone outside of the academic field for the position. Someone who understood marketing and communications.

"It's irrelevant that you probably know very little about what we do. You can learn that. And in doing so, you'll know what it is that the public and our donors will want to know. I'll send you a proposal by the end of the day," he said and ended the call.

Gemma was floored. This man wanted a professional and she was absolutely going to deliver. And the salary was more than she had been making. It would mean moving, meeting new people, adjusting to a new climate and new environment. Exciting, a little unnerving, but just the change she had been waiting for.

She made the move in January and by spring, Gemma was fully attuned to her new boss and workplace. Doctor Werner could turn the charm on when he wanted, but he was a difficult taskmaster, requiring everything to be rewritten and redone, usually just before the end of the workday. Luckily, although he was the most important researcher at Colter, he also held several administrative positions on campus and taught at least one graduate seminar that took him away from the lab in the woods on a daily basis. So, he wasn't in her face as much as he could have been.

However challenging her new job, she didn't regret the move for a moment. Well, perhaps for several moments when Valentine's Day came around and the only person she heard from was her father. The isolation of the lab deep in a forested area in Leesborough proper and not in the town didn't afford her the opportunity to interact with many people, either. The researchers and grad students who came and went seemed to consider her an oddity, and the only person she had any connection with was Mary Lemoyne, secretary to Doctor Allen, the actual director of Colter.

Even that relationship was situational only in that they ate their packed lunches together in the common room since there were limited dining choices in Leesborough and Gemma wasn't about to drive back to her apartment for a meal. Their conversation was amiable but generic once Gemma realized that their backgrounds and tastes were different. Mary seemed intrigued with Brooklyn and New York, having seen the movie *Gangs of New York* despite Gemma's reassuring her that it was no longer like that.

"Well, we don't have gangs down here," Mary said once. "Maybe in Raleigh, but not out here."

That was said with a nod indicating that, since Gemma technically lived in Raleigh, she might become prey to gang violence.

"I'm very careful," Gemma said. "Only quiet students live in my small complex."

"The ones with laptops and bikes that people like to steal. Never open the door to anyone you don't know," Mary advised.

"I have very secure locks on my apartment door."

"You should get a big dog. With a deep, loud bark."

"I don't know that my neighbors would appreciate that. And I certainly don't want to leave a dog all by himself all day."

Mary leaned in closer. "Do you know that some of the professors on campus actually bring their animals to work with them? Isn't that strange? We have two big ol' dogs at home and I can't imagine hauling them into work each day. Besides, Doctor Allen wouldn't allow it with all the precious animals here. You should have seen him during COVID. He was certain that someone was going to infect one of the monkeys."

"That's interesting because one of the theories about the virus was that it was transmitted from some animal species in a market in China to a human being."

"That's not what I heard. I read that a Chinese lab was experimenting with it and somehow someone got sick and brought it out to the city and then the rest of the world."

"Hmm," Gemma said, knowing that Mary hadn't read that but had seen a report on a news show or some website. These differences in perspective made even what little contact she had with Mary awkward at times.

While Gemma had spent the first months getting used to her job, her new boss, the workings of the center, its relationship to the university and her media contacts, she resolved to somehow put a face to the names to whom she sent press releases. It was time to make some coffee dates with those folks and develop her own network. Although she knew everyone at the Center by sight and some by name, they were still stand-offish with her, almost dismissive. Then, as the semester was coming to an end in spring, the atmosphere at the Center shifted even more and she sensed the tension of the grad students, some of whom were looking for job placements or fellowships.

Once, coming around a corner she heard raised voices, snatches of arguments that stopped when she appeared and there were slammed doors and whispers. She overhead someone mention Walter Benson's name and not in a kind way, although she couldn't quite put her finger on what caused the antagonism. One day Doctor Werner passed by her office, briefcase in hand, his face like thunder. He went into his large double office that he shared with his wife, and from the crashing sound must have hurled the briefcase at his desk.

"Something has to be done with that viper!"

Chapter 2

Everything changed one morning. As usual, Gemma drove the bumpy dirt road that snaked through the forest from the turnoff just a mile from Leesborough. Although it was humid and overcast, there must have been extensive traffic judging from the dust that had been kicked up. A bit beyond an opening in the forest, she went left onto a graded gravel road, then drove a little less than half a mile to the gatehouse. The one-person structure had been deserted long ago due to budget cuts, with grass growing close to the concrete and no one at the open gate, which would normally have been closed across the path. The heavy canopy of trees cast so much shade, the deep depressions in the road were almost invisible until she was right on top of them, jostling her car back and forth.

She bounced slowly along the lane, one car-width wide, and in places the forest begrudged even that space, with green saplings whipping the sides of the vehicle. It was an old-growth forest with enormous loblolly pines thrusting high into the sky, giving an oppressive feeling of darkness this early in the day. She wondered why the Colters, who had bought up this area from the proceeds of their pharmaceutical firm, had never exploited this vast area of pines and poplars, so valuable in the lumber trade.

Every few hundred feet a semicircle had been cleared to the left or right of the road to allow a vehicle to pass, although she met none coming out. Ahead, on a slight rise in the middle of the forest, was a clearing dotted with magnolia trees that always reminded her she was in the South. They framed the two-story building with its multiple wings that looked incongruous in the dense vegetation. The upper parking lot was full of cars, some of them marked police cars; an ambulance and the County Medical Examiner's van were parked at the service entry one story below.

Gemma parked her car, her heart racing at the thought that someone had been felled by a heart attack in the early morning. She was stopped at the entrance by a uniformed Leesborough police officer who asked for her identification but made no response to her inquiry about what was going on. She went into the chilly building and saw no one seated behind the reception desk. Not surprising; budget cuts from last year. It was quiet inside except for the low hum of the air conditioning. Further down a short hall she saw a small group of students talking in soft tones. As she approached to ask what was going on, they dispersed, and she looked down the corridor to the wing where the door stood open.

Along one side of the hall she was about to walk down was the cage where the lone rhesus that was unable to be socialized into any group was standing on his hind legs, looking in her direction. She tried not to make eye contact,

9

knowing that when she came within a few feet of the cage, the monkey would bare his teeth and scream repeatedly. He didn't disappoint, and her heart skipped a beat at the auditory onslaught, but she was careful not to alter her stride down the grey-tiled hallway.

"Miss," said a uniformed cop to her at the door to the wing at the end of the corridor.

"Yes," she mumbled, fishing out the identification on a lavalier that had slipped inside her blazer and showing it to him. He waved her in.

Inside she was hit with the dense, musky smell of animals and was temporarily stunned by the lack of light, which momentarily made her stop. As her eyes became accustomed to the gloom, she saw the door to one of the rooms was open and its light shone into the central area and across the jacket of a tall Black man with a wide, athletic back. His huge hands moved gracefully in the air as he spoke to Beatrice Werner and the janitor, Henry Simmons. A police lab tech in a white hazmat suit was carefully dusting the door jamb, the handles and a large stick with a key attached hanging nearby.

The big man put out his arm to prevent her entry as another man with reddish brown hair sidled past her, taking crime scene gloves from his jacket pocket and pulling them on before making his way through the open door of the room. Beyond the chain link antechamber was a tall cage with jungle gym-type equipment in it and an enormous, branched tree without leaves. The entire floor was covered with sawdust and at his feet, in the sawdust, lay a body. It was on its stomach with its feet towards the door and Gemma could see a track in the sawdust where it may have been pulled back to its current position.

One of the techs was shooting photographs of the cage and then closer images of the body and surrounding sawdust. Gemma stared as the officer stood for a moment, watching as someone else in a white hazmat suit kneeled on the ground and began to encase the hands.

Gemma gasped as she saw it was Walter Benson who lay before them.

The two men turned their heads in her direction and the man who was not entirely covered from head to toe approached her, concern on his face.

"I don't think you should be in here, Miss," he said with that soft Piedmont accent she had come to know in her short time in North Carolina.

He put his hand on her arm and guided her back out to the corridor.

"Are you all right?" he asked her, his eyebrows pulled together and his grayish blue eyes intent on her face.

"I'm not going to faint, if that's what you thought." She looked at his ID tag, which read Thibault.

"I'm making no assumptions," he said.

"Officer Tybalt?" she asked, pronouncing his name like the character in Romeo and Juliet.

"Tee-bow, as people say it here."

"Good. I'm Gemma Farnese, the public information officer."

"Thank you," he said. He looked down at his gloved hand and decided not to offer it to shake. "You're going to be hit hard today because of this." He turned back to the scene behind him.

Gemma approached Beatrice and the janitor. "What happened? What was he doing in there?"

"We don't know," Beatrice said. "You know it is entirely against protocol to enter the enclosure while the animal is still in there."

"I think he was trying to see if Z had gone into labor," Henry said.

"That might very well be, but dangerous for her and for him," Beatrice said.

"Where is she now?" Gemma asked.

"Henry opened the door to the outside run. She was very agitated, as you can imagine. Stupid, stupid boy," she muttered. "We ought to go back upstairs and let them do their work."

Beatrice left, with only Henry and Gemma observing the scene.

"Hey, T," the tall police officer said.

"Hey, Murph. "What do we got here, Conroy?" Thibault lifted the body's wrist with his gloved thumb and forefinger and looked carefully at the hand before the tech took it back.

"He got coshed on the back of the head. See there?" Conroy pointed to the right upper part of the skull farthest away from Thibault. There was blood on the head and neck and on the back shoulders of the tee shirt. "Lots of grey matter," he added pointing to a wet spot a few feet away.

"Hit with what?"

"Don't know yet."

Thibault turned briefly to the janitor. "Is this the key to this room?"

Henry Simmons nodded, and Thibault said to one of the Leesborough techs who was packing up. "Maybe you ought to take that key stick thing back with you to the lab."

"You bet."

"And check his pockets for keys and a cell phone." Thibault looked around him and then down at the body. "Who was he?" he asked Murphy.

"He's a student named Walter Benson." Gemma answered.

"Looks like some kind of stealth job. He hid his car in the trees at the edge of the parking lot," Thibault said. He looked back at Gemma, glad she had added that information but not entirely sure whether he wanted her to remain or not. He pointed to the wet spot and then back at the body. "What gives?" he asked Murphy.

"Seems like everybody was in here this morning. Body was originally back there," he said pointing toward the wet spot. "But he got drug out to over here by the janitor. Turned over onto his back. Then, when determined to be expired, turned *back over* onto his face."

"Great," Thibault said. "Why're you here, by the way? Where's Mutt?" He looked around for his partner, who would have gotten a separate phone call at home that morning at about the same time he had.

The Assistant ME and one of the techs were struggling with a body bag. "Didn't anyone call you? Mutt had emergency hemorrhoid surgery last night."

Thibault winced. "No one told me." Then he remembered someone had called from a number he didn't recognize and naturally he thought it was spam. It must have been Mutt's wife, whose number he didn't have in his contacts.

"So, are you with me on this one?" Thibault asked.

Murphy smiled broadly, then pulled his mouth down in mock sympathy. "Sorry, just here for the ride today. Too many vacations at once, you know. But let's talk to Gustafson. Maybe we can work something out."

"Vacations. Don't I know it. I'm supposed to take one week after this."

"Good luck, buddy. But I've got to get back to the office. You want to talk more to Mr. Simmons here?"

"Yeah, thanks. You all done?" he asked Conroy.

"That's it," the Assistant ME responded and zipped up the bag. "Here are keys, debit card, couple of bills but no phone." He handed them to Thibault, who put them in a plastic bag. While the techs pulled a gurney inside the room and loaded the body bag onto it, Conroy took his surgical gloves off with a snap. The techs wheeled past the janitor, who was now the only person in the corridor. The Leesborough Police Department had a few techs, in the event of a murder, but they relied on the County Medical Examiner's Office, which was better staffed and funded.

"I expect you want to talk with me," the janitor said, moving quietly towards Thibault, working his lips in and out of his mouth.

"Sure, just a couple of questions," Thibault said in a friendly tone. His glance down the hall showed him the back of the young woman moving swiftly toward the central stairs. He led the janitor away from the smell of the animals to the well-lit corridor and pulled a small, worn notebook out of his jacket pocket. But before he could ask anything, the man began speaking.

"My name's Henry Simmons." He pointed to his name embroidered on the gray work shirt. "I come in at seven a.m. every day like clockwork."

"Weekends, too?"

"No, not the weekends. Monday through Friday, seven to four. I empty the trash, sweep the floors, mop, clean up and stuff."

"Are you usually the first one here?"

"Oh, yes, sir. I'm usually the only one here for a long while."

Thibault looked at the monkey group outside the window. They seemed to be in the same positions as when he had first passed them.

"How did your day begin today?"

"Well, Z's expecting," he began. "The chimp. That's her cage there. She's due to have the baby any day. Anyhow, there's a pool on: whoever guesses the right day and time gets something, and the first to see the new baby gets something, too. So, I've been checking her cage pretty regular. Anyhow, this morning I went in, and I go directly to this wing, climbed the stairs—."

"Stairs?" Thibault interrupted. He walked back towards the wing, notebook in hand, and opened the door.

"Over there." Simmons pointed to a set of black metal steps in the gloom at the back of the room. He climbed the stairs, motioning Thibault to follow, and they emerged onto an expanse overlooking each of the animal enclosures with tinted windows through which the animals could be observed.

Simmons pointed. "See, you can see real good from up here. Downstairs you can only see through the little window in the door."

"What's all this?" Thibault asked of the chairs and tables positioned in front of each window.

"That's where they do what they call 'observing.' There are usually students up here most of the time watching and recording what the animals are doing."

"Including Walter Benson."

"Yes, him, too, sometimes."

"Why would Walter Benson be in the cage, especially if there is no animal in there?"

"Oh, there was, she was in there. I don't know what he was doing, they're not ever supposed to go in the cages. They are allowed sometimes in the outside space, between the door and the chain link, you know."

"Okay, now I am confused a bit. Where is the animal now?"

"She's outside. There is a switch, and it opens a door there, see? The door leads to a big area outside. I opened it and let her out."

"Start over. What happened when you came in here? Exactly what did you see?"

Simmons took a deep breath. "Okay. I came up here and looked through this big window and I couldn't see her in her usual corner or up in the tree. Z has been pacing back and forth a lot lately. It's usually a sign the birth is coming soon. They get restless just beforehand. I've seen more births than anybody here, I can tell you that. So, I got closer to the window and saw she was just kinda below me and bent over something darkish. It was a body lying on the floor."

"What position was Walter Benson in?"

"Face down, like this." Simmons put up his hands, his head to one side and closed his eyes. He stood there for a few seconds.

"And what did you do?"

"I ran down the steps, flipped the switch and let her out. Once I pulled the switch, she got out, fast. She must have been scared by me yelling and crashing down the stairs. I went into the cage and pulled him back towards the chain link area. But I stopped, because then I thought I better not move him anymore. Then I called Dr. Werner at home to tell him, and he said Dr. Beatrice was already on her way in."

"Whoa!" Thibault held up his hand. "Who is Dr. Beatrice?"

"Dr. Beatrice Werner. She's the lady with the dark hair who was here just a bit ago."

"Okay, what then?"

"Well, I came back in and turned him over to see if he was breathing, but I could already tell he was not. He also had blood and sawdust all over his face and up his nose."

"Okay, then what?"

"Then I turned him back onto his face." He and Thibault looked at each other a moment.

"Because?"

"Because I know you're not supposed to move the body."

Thibault raised his eyebrows and wrote a little more, thinking to himself, *but you did move the body.*

"Did you call the police?"

"Oh, no, Dr. Werner always told me to call him first if anything was the matter. He said he would call the police himself."

Thibault shook his head. "Wait a minute, you said 'him.' How many Dr. Werners are there?"

"Two: Dr. Klaus and Dr. Beatrice. They're married."

Thibault asked, "What time did you call him?"

"I don't know, maybe seven-fifteen?" It was more a question than a statement, and Simmons licked his lower lip.

"And when did Dr. Beatrice get here?"

"Right after, maybe seven-twenty, I guess."

Thibault looked down and saw Simmons was not wearing watch.

"Is there a clock in here?"

"No, there's one in the hall right above the door, though. That's how I knew what time it was. Dr. Beatrice came right down here to look in on Z, just as I did. She thinks the world of these animals. She saw me, and I told her what happened and I had called Dr. Klaus. She looked in the cage and she was incredibly upset, shaking like. She wanted to know if he was still alive, so she went in and, um—."

"Turned the body over," Thibault supplied.

"Yes, turned him over, wiped some of the sawdust from his face and put her hand on his neck to check his pulse. Then she put her head on his chest to check his breathing."

"Nothing?"

"Nothing."

"Then she went to call 911."

"But the body was face down when 911 got here, right?"

"Well, yes, I remembered you're not supposed to move the body."

"But you did move the body. A lot."

"I mean from how it was when I first found it," Simmons added.

Thibault was tired of being in the upstairs area, which was becoming increasingly stuffy, so he led the way down the stairs. Their footsteps clanged on the metal steps like a soundtrack of a submarine movie.

"Was it unusual for Dr. Beatrice to be here so early in the morning?" Thibault asked as they moved back out into the brightness of the corridor.

"Oh, no, she comes in early almost all the time. Sometimes just after me, sometimes before." Simmons was squinting at him in the bright light.

"I thought you said you were always the first one out here," Thibault said.

"Oh yes. Of the work crew. They come in about eight a.m. to get the animals' food ready. But Dr. Werner, him or her, lots of times they're here before me. Sometimes one of the researchers is out here all night observing. Lots of times Dr. Allen, he lives up the road, he'll check in on a sick animal in the early morning."

"Thanks, Mr. Simmons. I may need to ask you some other questions later. Can you tell me who is the manager of the building here? Who runs this place? The Werners?"

"Oh, no, that's Dr. Allen. His office is upstairs right along here, I'll show you."

The cement steps at the base of another wing took them to the second story almost right outside Allen's office. Thibault could see a thickset, bearded man standing with arms folded, talking to a woman behind the upstairs reception desk.

Henry Simmons pointed and turned to go back down the stairs.

"One more thing," Thibault said. Simmons stopped on the third step and turned back to face him. "Why did you pull Walter Benson out of the cage if you had already let the chimp out of the room?"

"I don't know. I wasn't thinking straight. I could see his brains were kinda leaking out."

Chapter 3

Dr. Allen turned his muscular upper body away from the window and watched Thibault as he approached. Thibault introduced himself and Dr. Allen extended a large hand in return. "Victor Allen. What can I do for you?" He scowled, drawing his ruddy brows down over piercing brown eyes.

"If we could talk a few minutes," Thibault said.

Allen stuffed his hands in his pants pockets and said gruffly, "Terrible business. Awful." He stopped and turned to look at Thibault more closely. "You weren't one of the guys out here last year, were you?" He had an aggressive tone to match his body, which looked as if he had been a collegiate wrestler.

"What about?"

"Those damned Animal Freedom activists. Somehow, they got onto the grounds and spray painted their liberating messages all over the buildings. Idiots. Cost me two and a half grand to repaint and clean up the mess."

"No, I wasn't out here. I had forgotten about it, as a matter of fact."

Allen looked at him quizzically, as if the event were so widely known that Thibault should have immediately remembered it. He led the way into his office and dropped noisily into a leather chair behind a cluttered teak desk. He motioned to the chair opposite for Thibault. Off to one side of the desk were floor-to-ceiling windows overlooking part of the lawn and magnolias in front of the building and the forest beyond. Directly behind his desk was a wall of bookshelves with a decorated coconut face positioned above Allen's own and bearing a remarkable resemblance. There was a collection of wind-up toy animals: a gorilla, an alligator, a chicken, a yellow-and-black snake, and a whole line of Godzillas in different colors on the topmost shelf. Thibault wondered if students had brought these for him, or a wife or a girlfriend. His own former girlfriend had gotten him a frog once—some forgotten joke—and now there was a whole shelf of them in the living room. Just looking at the array of jokey knickknacks made him decide he needed to pack up those tacky frogs and use the space for something else.

"I'll be heading the investigation of the death of Walter Benson for now, so I'd like to keep the lines of communication as open as possible. We'll keep you informed as to what's going on at all times," Thibault said.

Allen raised his hand in acknowledgement and then rested it on his cheek and combed his auburn beard with thick fingers. No wedding ring.

"Do you have Walter Benson's family's address or phone number by any chance?"

"Mary," Allen bellowed, "We got Benson's parents' number?"

A voice from the desk near the entrance yelled back, "No. Try Dean of Students."

"Good idea," Allen said.

Great, Thibault thought, rubbing the bridge of his nose. I can see we'll be butting heads all the way.

"Do you have a list of all those people who have keys to the buildings or gates?" Thibault asked.

"Mary, we got a list of everyone with keys?" Allen yelled again.

"Yes," she yelled back.

"Thirdly," Thibault continued, "although it's not necessary, I would be grateful for a spare office where I could question some of the people here in privacy. I think y'all would feel more comfortable, and it might be easier if I did some of it here instead of back at the Leesborough station."

"Wait, I thought the County was dealing with this?" Allen asked.

"Yes, they're doing the heavy lifting, but Colter is still within Leesborough jurisdiction."

"In that case, good idea. Then he yelled again, "Mary, we got a spare room?" There was no answer, but a short pause and Mary appeared at the door to the office. She was short, solidly built, middle-aged and had carefully styled hair.

"A what?" she asked.

"An extra office that, um, he could use."

Thibault interrupted and introduced himself to Mary Lemoyne.

"Well, Dr. Winkelman is gone until next month. I don't think he would mind." Then she added, "I just can't believe it about poor Walter. It's just awful. What do you think happened?" She crossed her arms over her ample chest and looked at Thibault with concern.

"Of course, we don't know quite yet."

"You don't think it was those Animal Freedom people who broke in here, do you? They wouldn't do a thing like that, would they?" She looked from Dr. Allen to Thibault.

"Why, had they actually broken into the building before?" Thibault asked.

"We have an alarm system on the building," Allen said. "And security cameras since that happened."

Cameras, Thibault noted mentally. That would help immensely.

"Yes, but—," she began.

Thibault looked expectantly at her. She looked back and forth at the two of them and cleared her throat.

"Had they come into the building before?"

Mary sidestepped the question. "It's just that a lot of people know the code. With a key to the building and the code, you're in. And Henry said the power was off when he came in, so there might not be footage to look at." She looked at Allen. "Sorry."

Allen stood up, slapping both palms on his desk. "Anything

else we can do for you just now?" he said, a little too loudly.

"As a matter of fact," said Thibault, still seated, "I'd like to talk to you for a few minutes." Mary moved quickly out of the doorway and shut the door behind her.

Allen sat down again and put incongruously small feet clad in running shoes on top of the desk. "Shoot." He raked his hand through his beard from ear to chin.

"What time did you get out here today?"

"Me?" Allen smiled, showing square teeth with spaces between them. "I'm always here. I live up the road less than a quarter of a mile." He jerked his thumb in the direction behind him.

"I didn't know there were any houses out here," Thibault commented.

Victor Allen chuckled. "Perk of the job. There's a tidy little house that is mine to use and, well, that's where I live. Easy commute." He gave what passed for a smile.

"Were you in the building last night?"

"Sure, I stopped in to check on Z. Nothing going on. All quiet here."

"And did you come back again during the night?"

"Nope." He raked his beard again, and some papers on the desk distracted him.

"Did anyone drive by your house last night or early this morning? Did you hear anything unusual?"

Allen returned his attention to Thibault. "My house is at the end of the road. Nobody drives past me to get in here.

The road you came in on is the only entry by car. Besides, if someone had come through in a tank, I wouldn't have heard it. I wear earplugs and have a white noise machine on in order to sleep. The only reason I heard the commotion this morning was because I was out watering my vegetable garden."

"What did you hear?"

"Lots of screaming. Animal screaming," he clarified. "From what I hear, Henry was yelling, and the animals got pretty excited, and they got each other going. They usually do that only if they see a hawk or a fox in the forest that comes too close to the outside cages. They can't get into the cages, mind you. In any case, it was pretty loud, so I came over to see what it was all about. Beatrice was already here."

There was a brief knock on the door and Mary gave a piece of paper to Dr. Allen, who glanced at it and handed it to Thibault. It was a list of the people who had keys to the building. Mary left, pulling the door closed behind her.

"There you go," said Allen, standing up again.

Thibault remained seated. "What time was that?"

Allen blew out his cheeks and answered, "About seven-thirty maybe." I wasn't fully dressed—didn't have my watch on, at least. I'm guessing from the clocks when I got into the building."

"Dr. Allen, what was Walter Benson doing inside an animal's cage in the middle of the night or early morning?"

"You got me. Strictly against policy. I would have booted him out if I had known."

"Do you mean: asked him to leave? Or asked him to leave the program? Could anyone else have 'booted him out'?" Thibault asked.

Allen sat back down. "As Director, I alone have authority to allow or deny people the use of the facility. As director of a funded project, or rather, projects, Dr. Werner can certainly make recommendations as to who can and who cannot have access to the building." This sounded like well-trod ground. Allen continued, "Walter Benson was a regis-tered graduate student at the University, with an approved research proposal, a negative TB test and up-to-date COVID vaccinations, among other inoculations. He met the criteria of eligibility according to the Colter Primate Center's policies as spelled out in our handbook." He leaned sideways to open a file drawer in his desk, extracted a folder, and slapped some stapled sheets constituting the handbook onto the desktop.

"Thanks," Thibault said, picking it up and shuffling it underneath the list. "Back to the chimp a minute. What is the likelihood Z could have killed Walter Benson?"

Allen exhaled and raked his beard. "Pregnant chimp. No one else around. I don't know. He could have startled her —she may have freaked. She wouldn't be happy, that's for sure. It's hard to say. She might have reacted if she had felt threatened. But attack? Dunno. Not likely."

"I thought I read somewhere chimps hunted?"

Allen guffawed. "Oh sure, we're talking rarely and only birds or small monkeys. And conspecifics." He swiveled his chair around to the bookshelf behind him. "Let's see—." He scanned the shelves for a reference.

"I thought Jane Goodall reported actual warfare between groups."

Allen said, "A little knowledge is a dangerous thing." He continued to scan the shelves.

Thibault didn't appreciate the comment. "Could someone have trained the chimp to attack?"

"Now where the hell did you get an idea like that?" Allen swiveled back around. "The days of teaching a chimp to smoke a cigarette, wear a suit and ride a bicycle are over, I hope. Our animals are used for breeding experiments and observation purposes only. Interaction with humans is kept to a minimum. To train an animal to do something like that would take so many hours and days—well, it couldn't be done without someone here seeing you do it. Ridiculous." He scowled as Thibault got up.

"It was just a question," Thibault said. He opened the door for himself, and Dr. Allen did not get up.

"Mary," he yelled. "Show him Winkelman's."

Winkelman's office was on the other side of the main entrance and had the same floor-to-ceiling windows as Dr. Allen's office. It had book-filled shelves, several large, potted tropical plants and bird photos on the walls. He drew open the net curtains and saw this office overlooked forest only, probably the choicest office in the building. The desk was teak and devoid of everything except a telephone. Thibault sat down and looked over the short list of names on the sheet he had brought in. He glanced at his watch and wrote down times alongside each name and then went back out to Mary's desk.

"Do you mean only these people have keys?" he asked.

"Oh, yes. We limit the number of keys. These are valuable animals here, you know. Of the people who come in daily, only Henry has a key. The others come in after him, Dr. Werner or Dr. Allen anyway. And we only give them to students with long-term research projects who may need to be here outside of normal working hours. We have so many visiting Fellows, you see. And of course, the admin staff. Like me."

Thibault asked if Mary could call the people on the list for them to come in at the times he had indicated in the margin. She pursed her lip as if considering whether she had reason to argue or comply.

"I don't think I have to call Ty and Paige. They just came in. Is it all right if I schedule them for noon?"

He looked at the list. Tyler Phillips and Paige Hammond.

"Okay, thanks. Is there someone who can give me an orientation of this place? Layout and so on?"

Chapter 4

Mary directed him to the Public Information office. Essentially the building was a two-story square with corridors along the outside of the square and offices on the inside, many of which faced an interior courtyard. A wing extended from each corner of the building; these were also two stories high but accessible only from doors on the first-floor corridor.

He found the Public Information office, knocked and was asked to come in. He stepped in and Gemma, her back to him at first, turned quickly, her hair swinging briefly into her face. It was a smallish office but it did have a tall window with a view of the forest that made it seem much larger. She stood up, a cell phone to her ear, and motioned for him to sit down. He caught the scent of jasmine as she leaned towards him, a scent evoking two powerful and pleasant memories: his grandmother's porch swing at the farm when he sat next to her, and much later, necking with some girl in his brother's car on warm summer nights down by the dam. A little embarrassed by both her proximity and the intensity of the memories, he looked down and flipped through his notebook.

Switching the phone to her other ear, she sat down and smoothed the front of her skirt while she spelled names aloud, gave dates and cited figures she had on printed sheets before her in a quick, precise voice, noticing that he was taking in the surroundings in a discreet way. As she continued talking, she moved her head from side to side indicating that it might be a long conversation, so he stood up to look at the contents of the office. While he scanned the room, she checked out his broad back and when he turned, his aquiline nose and unruly hair.

He glanced at the open laptop on the desk and a tall file cabinet beside it with a printer on top. Bookshelves along the wall held stacks of Colter Primate Center brochures and potted plants. Across the room on the other wall were large, framed photos of the Center and animals and smaller photos of what appeared to be dignitaries shaking hands in posed promotional photos.

Gemma finished her conversation, stood and said, "You know, when I saw you downstairs, I thought you might be with the media until you put on your gloves. This is so awful. Do you know what happened?" She motioned him to sit again, and she sat, leaning towards him inquisitively.

His face was tanned—an outdoor sort of guy.

"Just what you may have overheard. We won't begin to know until the autopsy is done."

"His poor family. I guess he had some family." Then she added, "There seemed to have been a lot of blood."

"Yes, there was a fair amount," he said, nodding his head.

"Fair? No, I meant there was quite a bit."

He paused to stare at her. "That's what I just said."

"Okay." She was confused by his wording and then leaned over her shoulder and looked at a door to an adjoining room, her hair swiveling with the motion. Leaning in toward him again, she said in a soft voice, "Someone said—."

The door behind her opened suddenly and she stood quickly. A tall, middle-aged man with short, blond hair stared at them.

"Who the devil are you?" he directed at Thibault. He put his head back slightly as if to get a better look at him.

"Dr. Werner, this is Sergeant Thibault of the Leesborough Police. Sergeant, Dr. Werner," Gemma provided, hoping to ease the discomfort.

Werner shook his hand and exhaled in relief. "Oh, Sergeant, how good of you to come up to see us. What a horrible business. So, so unfortunate." He clasped his other hand on top of the one already engaged.

"Yes, well, it's never pleasant. However, I hope we can do a thorough investigation to determine what occurred."

"I quite understand. Anything we can do to help. Anything."

Thibault disengaged his hand. "I would like a map of the Center, if you have one."

"Certainly, certainly. Gemma?" Dr. Werner looked expectantly at her. She nodded, squeezed past Thibault to look through a stack of papers on the bookshelf.

"And I or one of the other officers will be talking to everyone over the course of the next few days—."

"Naturally, naturally," Werner interrupted. Beatrice—my wife—is extremely upset by all this, as you can imagine we all are. She's taking it dreadfully hard." Rubbing his hands together, he continued, "Now, to begin with, I'll have Gemma give you a tour of the Center so you can become better oriented."

She put her head up quickly and glanced from one to the other over her shoulder and nodded.

"It will have to be short. It won't be long before the phones start ringing," she said. "I've already called the University's communications person and given them the heads up. But that doesn't mean the media won't be calling here."

Werner sighed, then took Thibault's hand again and shook it. "Will you excuse me?" He backed out into what was evidently his own, much larger office, and a gust of air riffled the papers on her desk.

"Would you like the standard PR slash Noted Dignitary tour or the modified Lesser Dignitary half-hour one?"

"My guess is I might fit into the Lesser Dignitary category. Changing the topic for a moment, did you know Walter Benson well?"

She pulled her head back slightly at the question. "Hardly at all. I mean, I knew who he was by sight and reputation."

"Which was?"

"What?"

"His reputation."

"That he was a researcher here," she answered. "Shall we go, Sergeant Steve?" she asked, putting her cell in the pocket of her blazer and holding up a map of the building. She led them to the hall and an elevator next to her office. She pushed the first-floor button, and they rode slowly down. "I was going to give you some deep background on the Colter Primate Center, but I probably don't have to if you're a local."

"Is it that obvious?" he asked without smiling. "And you. I take it that you aren't. Where are you from?"

"New Jersey," she said adding, "No New Jersey jokes, please."

"I'm afraid I don't know any New Jersey jokes."

It was her turn to stare at him.

"Let me guess, you've never spent any time in the South before, right?" he asked.

"Well, no, I mean if you don't count Miami or Palm Beach."

"We don't count them as being the South as a rule."

She smirked at his retort. "Spring break and stuff."

They passed several closed doors that were evidently not part of the tour.

"I've been here since January. Still getting acclimated, I guess. But it has been more of an adjustment than I thought. Am I talking too fast for you? Everybody around here comments on it."

"I can keep up," he said. He looked up and saw that security cameras were placed strategically in the corridor, providing wide surveillance. As long as they were functioning.

"You'd think that the security system would somehow be wired to operate in the event of an outage," he said.

"I wouldn't know. Dr. Allen might be able to answer that question."

She stopped in front of a floor-to-ceiling window facing a large yard where monkeys sat in groups or ambled around on the ground. "Colter Primate Center was started and endowed by Edmund Colter in the nineties to study breeding, social structure and mental health in primates as they related to humans. Did you know him?" she asked without a break in momentum, looking directly at him. Her eyes were dark green.

He wondered for a moment if it was a standard question she asked everyone to whom she gave the tour. "You can't grow up in Leesborough and not know who Edmund Colter was. However, our family didn't belong to the same country club," he added.

"Oh," she responded with a small smile, not quite understanding what he meant.

"It's an expression," he explained.

"Oh."

He could tell she had no notion of Edmund Colter's relationship to the folks there. Or that he once lived in a large house on the outskirts of town and had visited only a few times a year from Chicago. He called it The Farm. The only thing he held in common with the residents of Leesborough was that half of them worked on real farms and the other half worked in some capacity for Colter Pharmaceuticals.

She continued, "In recent years, because of Klaus Werner's work and many grants, hybridization and its effects on social structure have become an added focus. This is where Z comes into the picture. Have you seen her?" Gemma asked as she opened a door from the corridor to the surrounding forest. The humidity had increased since earlier in the morning, but it was still overcast. They stood outside the chain link fence of the wing with the outdoor area of Z's cage in front of them.

Gemma leaned against a pine tree and picked off a piece of sap and squashed it between two fingers. "Z's a rare animal, a bonobo. They used to call them pygmy chimps. *Pan paniscus*—terrific name, don't you think? Isn't she beautiful?" she added as the chimp looked back at them from a distance. The animal was smaller than he had expected and quite dark.

Thibault laughed briefly at Gemma's enthusiasm.

"I do," she resumed. "I think she's beautiful. These animals live in central Africa and not as many studies have been done on their social behavior compared to, you know, your everyday chimp. But they are a different species, and it has been assumed behavior plays a huge role in the maintenance of species lines."

Thibault looked sideways at her. "Did you know all this stuff already or did you have to learn it for this job?"

She shrugged and snapped her fingers with a smile. "I'm a quick study." She continued, "They tried to get her to mate with a common chimp, but no go. Well, I mean a *common chimp*—that's a hard sell. Anyway, did you know they are called *Pan troglodytes*? Isn't that a hoot? As if they lived in a cave. Well, he did act like a caveman. See the ear?"

Thibault noticed a ragged left ear, lighter than her face.

"Poor sweetie. Old Bert decided if they couldn't mate, they might as well fight. Anyway, they ended up doing artificial insemination. Hence, the long-awaited hybrid child. That all happened before I got here, of course."

Z got up and moved closer to the fence and walked slowly, leaning on her knuckles, while Thibault leaned down a bit to get a good look at her hands. She kept her eyes on him as she walked by and he could see the bulge of her abdomen then, which was a lot smaller than he had imagined for an animal about to give birth.

"I understand there's a pool to guess the birth date or be the first to see the baby," Thibault said. "Do you think it could have been the reason Walter Benson was in the cage with her?"

She shrugged. "I doubt it. Walter was difficult in many ways, but he was a serious researcher and wouldn't have gone in just to win a bet. Besides, you don't have to be a serious researcher to know not to get so close to something potentially dangerous."

"Why, has she ever hurt anyone?"

Gemma stammered a bit and then said, "When she first came here a few years ago—obviously, I was not here, it is just something I heard—evidently someone's arm got broken. I understand it had to do with sloppy handling.

That's off the record," she added, holding her finger up and widening her eyes for emphasis.

"I'm not a reporter," Thibault said.

"Well, I'm sure the injury wasn't intentional. She looks smallish but the proportion of the arms and shoulders compared to the rest of the body makes for a powerful animal. And now a pregnant and protective one."

Thibault felt the sweat beginning on his neck and swatted a gnat away from his face. Gemma was looking at the chimp again.

"I wonder what goes on in her mind sometimes. Does she see herself like a character in a romance novel, a captive princess, waiting to be rescued and taken back to her rightful kingdom?" She picked off another gob of sap and played with it, then smiled at her comment.

They walked back towards the door, their feet slipping on the dry, hot pine needles. "Sure wish it would rain," Thibault said. He suddenly felt it was a stupid thing to have said.

"Listen," Gemma put her hand on his arm.

Thibault heard the usual sounds of the forest.

"What a strange bird," she held her hand up again when it began again. "I've never heard anything like it."

"That's a mockingbird," Thibault said with a laugh. "Don't you have them up north?"

"If we do, I never paid much attention before. But I'm sure I would have recognized that bird call."

He paused, trying to tell if she were joking. "They are called mockingbirds because they imitate the sounds of other birds."

"Oh. It makes sense, I guess."

"Sometimes they imitate animal noises or mechanical sounds, too."

She looked at him out of the corner of her eye, trying to guess if he was joking, and then swatted a gnat that had come close to her face. "Have you noticed the warmer the climate, the more horrible the bugs and crawly things are?"

"You don't have insects up North? Hard to believe. Here, in the woods you have to look out for chiggers, too. Nasty." He shook his head for emphasis.

"Chiggers—are you making that up?"

"No, really."

"What do they look like? Have you ever been stung by one?"

"They bite. They get in under your skin and it's real hard to get them out. People put nail polish on top to suffocate them."

She looked at him out of the corner of her eye again, shook her head slightly as if not quite believing what he said and opened the door to the hall. She glanced at her watch and picked up the walking pace as they proceeded to the interior of the wing. Over the entry door was a clock and Thibault noticed it was five minutes faster than his watch.

"You can see into the rooms from down here, but real observation takes place upstairs or outside," she explained.

"The anterooms are for animal handlers or staff for feeding. In this wing we have some macaques, green monkeys, colobuses, and spider monkeys."

She turned suddenly. "I hope you don't think I am being callous about Walter Benson—not being more upset or something. I really didn't know him at all, practically."

"But you said he was difficult."

"Did I?" She turned away and continued walking around the interior of the wing, pointing out the species and names of the animals, and then led them out to another corridor facing the outdoor area Thibault had seen earlier. The lone monkey in the hall cage screamed and lunged at them from behind his bars.

"Rhesus macaque," Gemma said. "Backbone of the place in many ways because they've been so intensely studied and written about. And experimented on, frankly. Bruce is one of the maladjusted ones. Brought up motherless as part of some horrible experiment at some other facility and then palmed off as a viable male. As you can see, he has some serious interpersonal issues." They continued walking towards the further wing. "We've got about six indoor rooms, several small outdoor runs as well as a one-acre area with rhesus in them." They passed closed doors. "Meeting rooms. More labs." Each time she turned to say something to him, her hair swung across her face momentarily.

"This wing is my favorite; all the really strange animals live here." She opened the door and walked around the interior perimeter, looking in at rooms of mostly sleeping animals. She stopped at one window and leaned on the ledge. "How amazing to be abducted and spirited thousands of miles away from your home."

"Do you usually say these things on your tour?" he asked.

She smiled. "No. I don't know what's got into me today. Aren't these wonderful names: the aye-aye, Hapalemur, those, there. Those little guys are mouse lemurs; a pair of proboscis monkeys and I don't know who just got moved in here. She looked in and said, "I don't know who these guys are. The nameplates on the door haven't been updated yet."

As they proceeded from one wing to another, Gemma waved an arm to the left and right. "Kitchens, food storage, food preparation, maintenance and shop." They stood next to the door where he had come in earlier. "Upstairs are several rooms of animal records and computers for input and retrieval of same.

"This wing is kind of dull. Galagos, mostly, and other nocturnal animals so we try to keep out of there during the day so as not to disturb their sleep. I guess I think they are dull because I'm not here at night. It doesn't help they smell particularly noxious, and they also bite."

"Is that what the gloves hanging in the wings are for?"

"Oh, yes. But largely ineffective. At least the gloves take most of the force of the bite and protect from breaking the skin. But it hurts like hell all the same, so I'm told. Dr. Werner tried to get me to do some animal handling early on so I would have the full experience, as he put it, but he was probably just showing off and hoping some animal would take a hunk out of me. We had a difficult day, as I remember. But I didn't need to get bitten to appreciate how demanding handling the animals can be."

"You aren't telling me someone tries to catch a monkey in those big butterfly nets I saw, are you?"

"I'm not pulling your leg. That's how they do it."

Thibault looked at her askance, and she smiled.

"Really," she said more earnestly.

She walked quickly towards another wing, and he followed. The corridors had only native forest for a view, enclosed by chain link fencing.

"Sick animals are quarantined down here so you get some ghastly sights from time to time. Upstairs is the carrel room with cubicles for students or out-of-town researchers to work on their notes or collaborate. It looks like a call center."

"For humans or the monkeys?"

She laughed. "Sure, they've hired all these monkeys at minimum wage, no benefits, naturally, to sell extended car warranties to the unsuspecting. That wing over there has all the big guys. Well, except for Z. There's Old Bert, the erstwhile father. Although he has done quite well siring some of his own kind, too, back at his old zoo."

"Aren't there any larger animals?" Thibault asked. "Like gorillas? Or orangs?"

"Colter is well funded, but the amount of additional space they would require as well as the liability would be prohibitive."

He looked at her for an explanation.

"Word would get out if we had orangs or gorillas and the security issue would be out of control."

"It may not have been very much in control already," he said.

She didn't respond as they continued walking along the corridor. "The fellows and postgrads come from all over while the grad students are from the University, with some from UNC and Duke. Not too many people here this late in the year, though. But wait until the cold weather hits up north, and we'll have a flock from the Universities of Chicago, Wisconsin and Michigan."

"Did the weather have anything to do with your decision to come here?" he asked.

"Hell, yes. I don't deny it. Have you lived out of this area much?"

"Northerly just to Boston in the summer and it was fantastic, and DC in the winter. It was surprisingly cold. And sometimes the summers there can be as hot and humid as here." They stopped.

"Upstairs is the Grand Old Man's office, Winkelman. He's in Africa negotiating to set up a permanent research station. Dr. Allen's office is up there, too. Would you like to meet him?"

"I have already. In fact, I'm due to be up there to talk to some other people soon."

She turned to face him squarely. "Well, that's the end of the tour. A bit longer than I intended." They walked toward the elevator.

"Sorry, didn't mean to keep you away from your work so long. Can I repay you with a late lunch?" he asked, looking down at his watch.

"I'm on call to answer any media questions for the rest of the day. But thanks anyway. They shook hands and had those awkward moments of silence as the elevator took them to the second floor.

"We can do a rain check," he added as she headed for her office and gave him a thumbs up.

Chapter 5

Mary told Thibault that Beatrice Werner had gone off to teach a class and attend to administrative duties at the University. He asked for her office and home numbers to set up an interview as soon as possible. Although the other officer, Murphy, had taken a preliminary statement from her, he had wanted to talk to her while her memories were still fresh. Now he had no choice but to wait.

Tyler Phillips stood looking at a framed bird print outside Winkelman's office. A tall, thin young man with long, dirty blonde hair, he wore jeans and an oversized green tee shirt. At the sound of Thibault's footsteps, he turned around, squinted, put his hand out and introduced himself. There was the odor of cigarette smoke about his clothes. Thibault gestured the way into the office and said, "This is just an interview, not an interrogation. I'm looking for background information on what might have happened. Still, if you would be more comfortable having legal advice available —," Thibault held out his hands in a non-threatening pose, and the young man appeared to consider the idea for a moment, but then shook his head. His hair flopped into his eyes, and he brushed it back.

"Let's sit down, Tyler," Thibault suggested.

"Ty."

"Okay, Ty. When did you get out here today?"

"Paige and I came in together about eight-thirty. We drove in together." The index and third fingers of his right hand had nicotine stains and he tapped them on his thigh erratically as he spoke.

"And where were you last night?"

"AT THE PARTY for Herb Pierce. The party at the Werners."

"Who is Herb Pierce?"

Ty looked startled. "Just one of the most important primatologists in the United States."

"Does he teach here?"

Ty snorted. "No, he's at Columbia. He was visiting, hence the party."

"Okay, when did you leave?"

"Paige and I left elevenish. We live together." He added, "We're getting married in the fall."

"Congratulations," Thibault said. "Did you come here to the Colter Center at any time during the night or early morning?"

"I don't do research here anymore. I finished my orals last month. I'll be relocating to California in a few weeks, so I've been spending time getting my stuff together for that."

"But you still have a key, according to this list." Thibault pulled the paper out and then wondered how many others were out there uncollected by the Colter staff.

"Well, yes, I do. Allen's been on my case to return it before I go. Don't worry, I will." He stood up and fished around in his jeans pocket and produced a key ring and started to take one of the keys off.

"Hey, no need," Thibault said as Ty put the key on the desktop and sat back down. "That's not my job." He looked back down at his notebook. "And you didn't come out here until this morning?" Ty nodded in response. "How well did you know Walter Benson?"

Ty shifted his weight in the chair, laced his hands and placed them on the desk. "Actually, we shared living quarters for a semester, until this past December." He looked Thibault in the eye.

"You were roommates? Did you get along?"

"Sure. But then he started this vendetta against Werner, and he got a bit unbalanced." He laughed nervously, showing badly crowded bottom teeth. "You should have seen him last night."

"What happened?"

"Walter created a scene at the party. Of course, he wasn't invited, so he crashed it. Called Werner names. Fraud, etc. Along those lines." He produced a thin smile.

"What was that all about?"

Ty sighed. "Walter had this idea Werner had made up some of his research or falsified it or something. I don't know. It was some conspiracy type of thing he had. I mean, there was no proof. Walter was always about to produce the proof, so he said. He's been saying it forever, so how could you take it seriously?" Ty slid his hands off the desk, leaving streaks of condensation behind.

"Are you close to Werner?"

"Well, sure. I mean we worked together a lot. Published a paper. He was my thesis advisor, for Chrissakes. We're not good buddies, if that's what you mean. Strictly professional relationship."

"How did he feel about Walter Benson?"

Ty shrugged. "Furious."

"I meant how did he feel about him in general?"

"You'd better ask him."

"What led to your moving out?"

"Paige and I decided to move in together before California and it just seemed the time was right."

"No argument with Walter? No difficulties? No fight?"

Ty scoffed. "Nope."

"Did you know anyone who would want to harm Walter Benson? Any enemies?" This was the question Thibault was instructed he must always ask, and it always felt over the top.

"A lot of people didn't warm up to him and he didn't go out of his way to win popularity contests, but enemies? That's a bit harsh."

"Besides Werner."

"I didn't say Werner was his enemy. You said that."

"Oh, you're right. Sorry," Thibault said as he flipped through some pages of his notebook as if he had lost his place. "Well, I guess I don't have any more questions right now." He stood.

Ty got up slowly.

"So where are you going in California?" Thibault asked as he opened the door.

"Paige has an appointment at Berkeley. I don't have a job yet, but I'll be working on finishing some papers and writing a book from my dissertation."

"What will it be about?"

"You wouldn't be interested," Ty responded as he walked away.

Same to you, buddy, Thibault thought. He walked out into the hall, stretched his back and rubbed his eyes. He went to the end of the corridor and looked out the window at a tall, wire mesh cage a short distance from the building. He looked down at gray, raccoon-like animals with ring-striped tails chasing each other from branch to branch on a large, dead tree trunk in the enclosure. Other animals sat on the ground in groups, ignoring the commotion above them. He had seen monkeys like this in a cage in one of the wings, but he couldn't remember what Gemma said they were called. A movement outside the cage caught his eye: someone was observing these animals from a bench nearby. A woman in loose-fitting shorts and shirt with a ponytail and a camp hat on was writing while looking at the animals and periodically looking at a watch. He wondered what was being written down, especially since the animals were engaged in the same activity for the few minutes he looked on. They just moved around. Was the observer making any sense of these movements? Was there any sense to be made of these movements, or just some human construct overlaid on random behavior?

It was obvious they could see the observer, but Thibault wondered if it made a difference in what they did or didn't do. Or were they oblivious to the human who sat there because they were dreaming of their homeland, waiting to be rescued, as Gemma suggested. He had to smile at the idea and now it made him wistful. Wistful about loss—what loss? He had his homeland, this was it. Only he wasn't sure it was all he wanted. He felt a pang of years of leading a conventional life, doing what was expected, not making himself happy and not really pleasing anyone else for all the effort. And in the end, it had been so simple to break off the engagement, so why hadn't he done it before? You just declare yourself free and start over. He felt someone looking at him, but it was just one of the animals. Its large eyes encircled with black made it seem startled but in reality, nothing—not the other animals racing by or a vehicle pulling up to the front entrance— seemed to faze it, perhaps dreaming of another life, too, on the other side of the cage.

When Thibault returned to Winkelman's office, he saw a young woman seated at a bench nearby, evidently waiting to talk to him. Must be Paige Hammond. Thibault lifted his eyebrows, and she got up and walked over to him. She held out her hand, and on her wrist was what he thought they called a tennis bracelet, a thin gold strand with small diamonds on it. Thibault couldn't imagine a more unlikely girlfriend for Ty Phillips. She looked more like a young suburban wife who had just popped in for a chat before lunch at the country club. She had on a blue, button-down oxford blouse tucked into chino pants and a headband holding her blonde, shoulder-length hair away from a slightly tanned forehead. What an odd couple; Ty didn't look like he had seen the outside sun or exercise in years.

She followed him into Winkelman's office, sat down, crossed her legs and put her purse on the floor beside her chair. She looked at him expectantly.

"I suppose you know why I asked to speak with you today," he said.

"Yes," she said. "It is really quite shocking and sad." She seemed to put some effort into it, but she didn't look particularly shocked or sad. Her voice had a trace of a Southern accent, Virginia, or South Carolina maybe, which made her comment seem a bit more sincere.

"When did you get in this morning?"

"About eight-thirty. I'm sure Ty told you that."

"And where were you last night?"

"Didn't Ty tell you? We went to the Werners' party." She had a small crease of concern between her eyes. Her eyes were light blue, matching her blouse, and she kept them focused on Thibault. "Oh, of course, we're supposed to tell it in our own words or something, right?"

"Or something. Where did you go after the party last night?"

"Ty and I went back home. I had had a long day escorting Herb Pierce around the University, so I was anxious to go to bed early."

"Who is this Herb Pierce?" Although he had already gotten the information from Ty, he wanted to hear what she had to say.

"Someone who was in town from Columbia, a big name in the field. We wanted to show him what we had here at Colter."

"Did anything unusual happen at the party?"

She looked up at the ceiling and seemed to be debating what to say.

"I understand there was some kind of accusations made by Walter about Dr. Werner."

"Oh, that," she said. "I didn't catch much of it since I was in the yard when the commotion began. Raised voices are primarily what I heard."

Thibault wrote in his notebook and let the silence accumulate, but she did not add anything to her comments.

"About what time did you get home?"

She looked up at the ceiling again for her answer, "About eleven, I would say."

"Did both of you go to bed at the same time?"

"Yes," she said, meeting his look.

"Did you come out here either last night or early morning?"

"No."

"What about Ty?"

"To the best of my knowledge, no."

Thibault digested this strange answer by writing something in his notebook.

"Who do you think might have wished Walter Benson harm?" he asked, looking up and meeting her gaze directly.

"I can't think of anyone doing something as violent as what seemed to have happened. It must have been a vagrant or something. Or maybe one of those animal rights activists, you know, Animal Freedom."

"The security cameras had been turned off. That would point to someone who knew how to deactivate them. A vagrant would need keys to the gates and the building and then have to figure out where the keys to the animals' rooms were kept and then search all the rooms in the building for someone to crack on the head. Come on now, a vagrant? And did the animal rights people have a vendetta against Walter in particular?"

Her face colored slightly, and she looked down. "Of course not. I don't know why I said that."

"That's neither here nor there. How well did you know Walter Benson?"

"Quite well, actually."

Finally, Thibault thought. Someone admits knowing the guy.

"Our parents are good friends in Atlanta, and it was because of me he came to the University for his graduate work."

"How's that?"

"I had worked with Klaus Werner at UC Davis, where he was before this. When I got to the University here, I had the rare privilege of working with the Jane Goodall Institute in the Gombe for my dissertation research. Naturally, Walter's parents knew about my academic work, but the ***Atlanta-Journal Constitution*** ran a cover story in its Sunday magazine about me and my research, complete with photos I had taken and sent home. In fact, the text was excerpts of a kind of diary I had kept and brought home. They were a 'Dear Mom and Dad' kind of letters, chatty, not academic at all." Her face colored again, and she continued.

"It's unusual to garner so much public notice for academic research, I assure you, but the Goodall name is always a draw. And the fact I was my high school's homecoming queen made for an interesting contrast. I think the attention and notoriety turned Walter's head a bit. He was at Emory at the time and decided to change his major and later enroll here as a graduate student."

"So, *you* encouraged him to come here?" Thibault asked.

"Oh, yes. His grades were very good, likewise his GREs and he was focused." She looked straight at him.

"But?"

"Well, he was always a bit full of himself. I don't know what happened, but he became adversarial with his professors."

He knew she was trying to lead him in another direction and not too subtly.

"He initially wanted to work with Winkelman, but just

before he got here, he decided he wanted to be Werner's protégé instead."

"Okay, now I'll ask you. What happened?"

She sighed a small sigh and the little crease between her eyes reappeared. "They got along famously at first, but Walter could sometimes be difficult, and I don't know how it came about, but they had a tremendous argument. They became—enemies. I'm sorry," she said hastily. "I don't know how else to put it. They took every opportunity to say nasty things about each other and each other's work. And Werner blamed me for it one time."

"That sounds ridiculous." He paused. "Why blame you?"

"I know! Werner wanted to blame someone, and he didn't dare lay it at Winkelman's door." She looked out the window over his shoulder for a moment. "I think the real problem with Walter was not the personality conflict with Werner. You see, this year when Walter turned twenty-one, he found out he was adopted. I know, hard to believe, isn't it? Crazy that his parents didn't tell him. Of course, none of us knew about it. They moved to Atlanta when he was small. Anyhow, he did not take it well."

"Hmm," Thibault muttered.

"He essentially stopped talking to his parents for a while. He directed a lot of animosity towards Werner, and he wasn't particularly pleasant to me, either. The whole business was trying. Anyway, no one believed the crazy theories Walter had—and was anxious to share—but he couldn't seem to stop digging a hole for himself."

"Did you try to talk to him about his behavior?"

She turned the bracelet so the clasp was under her wrist. "I felt it was my responsibility to do so. After all, it was partially on account of me he came here and it was certainly my fault, or so he put it, that Ty was moving out as his roommate. Maybe he felt he was being abandoned. I don't know. He was trying so hard to be unlikeable. I took him out to dinner. I tried to talk to him about keeping things in perspective. He didn't want to talk about it at all; he wanted to grill me about Werner's past instead. Then the usual harangue about truth and honesty and peoples' inability to face up to reality. He said he was close to getting verification about who his birth parents were and then I would see his point of view."

"What did that have to do with anything?"

She shrugged.

"How did his family react?"

"They supported him in his search. He took a DNA test but didn't come up with any matches. What else could they do? They continued to send him money each month, even though he wouldn't talk to them on the phone. I think they thought he would work through the anger eventually."

She laced her fingers in her lap and sat back. "I may have been the only person to whom he actually spoke to about his birth parents." She paused. "Sometimes adopted people have these fantasies about who their real parents are. It might not be someone famous, but it is usually something fantastic all the same: a Congressman, a movie star, a murderer, you know. Walter had a fantasy, too, although he called it an educated guess." She paused again. "He told me he strongly suspected Werner was his real father."

Chapter 6

After a morning in the eerily quiet and substantially air-conditioned Colter Primate Center, Thibault enjoyed the blast of humid air when he exited the building. His truck bounced along the rutted dirt road while his previous thought that its condition was a purposeful deterrent to the curious was replaced by the notion that perhaps the Center had financial problems. Although founded and presumably funded by the Colters, maybe their support had been waning in recent years, or whatever grants kept it going were drying up. 'Follow the money' was always good advice and could be the root of the motivation behind Walter Benson's being killed. What if those accusations he made of fraud had to do with financial malfeasance? As he rocked from side to side through the gullies and ditches of the roadway, Thibault knew it was always a strong motive although uncovering the morass of finances was a tedious, detailed job and not part of his skill set.

Rather than going to one of his usual lunch haunts, he decided to make his way towards Raleigh and any fast-food restaurant whose parking lot was not too full; he didn't want to wait, and he didn't want to run into anyone and have to make small talk.

It was a brief foray to the outside world, and after the bone-rattling ride back to the Center, Thibault once again sat in the cool of Winkelman's office, waiting for the first of the work staff to come in to be interviewed. He called Beatrice Werner's office on campus and was told by her secretary she had gone home ill. Trying her cell, she didn't pick up and he left a message. Then he called his own office to find out if anyone could help with the interviews the next day and spoke to Aileen, who was uncooperative about who might be available.

Back to interviewing.

The biggest problem he now faced was that most of the work staff, except for Henry Simmons and a dietician who showed up once a week, consisted of students who worked in return for tuition credits at the University. The jobs were highly sought after and Dr. Allen had maximized their number, possibly to help with scheduling, so there were about fifteen students who worked there on a part-time basis, some just a few hours a week. Thibault was only able to talk to three students who hadn't gone back to campus for classes. There was some time in tracking them down at the Center, and then the interviews went slowly, and he got no new information anyway. He was going to have to continue doing these for the next few days and probably into next week to cover everyone.

After what felt like a long, non-productive afternoon, Thibault called Mutt's cell and spoke to his wife, who was in the hospital waiting room. She said Mutt was in recovery and she would be taking him home as soon as they discharged him. He gave her well wishes and decided to wait until tomorrow to make a visit at their home. At that moment, he was looking forward to being in his own house with a cold beer when he remembered Assistant Chief Gustafson had lent him a book that he ought to return. He decided to put it on his desk today when he wouldn't be in his office. If he waited until tomorrow, Gustafson would have him sit down for an excruciating conversation about the merits of the book, which he hadn't wanted to read in the first place.

Back outside, he took off his jacket, loosened his tie and started to the truck. He went slowly out of the drive toward the stand of pines, where several cars were parked, and where Gemma stood violently kicking the tires on one of them.

Thibault pulled over and called out, "Need some help kicking those back to life?"

"Oh, the damned car died again," she called back.

He brought his vehicle to a stop and turned off the engine. "Let's see what the matter is," he said, looking for the hood release.

"I told you. It died," she said tersely.

"I can see that."

"I know what's wrong with it," she interrupted. "I just got it repaired the other day. Electrical voodoo." She waggled her hands in the air. "And they obviously screwed something up rather than fixing it. I called them already and they'll send someone out to tow it. And pay for the towing. And keep fixing it until they get it right." She gave him a tight smile.

"I'd be happy to look at it for you," he said calmly.

"Nope." She crossed her arms and kept the tight smile in place. "I should stay with the vehicle, but it's too warm out here and who knows when they'll show up. Keys are in the ignition, and obviously nobody can start it to steal it."

"Well, I'll carry you."

She stared at him. "What?"

"I mean, I'll give you a ride. Come on." He moved his jacket off the front seat, and she slid in beside him, a scowl on her face.

"Are you in a hurry?" he asked. "I've got to stop at my place right quick and pick something up. Where are you headed?"

"Back to town to my apartment." She tossed her head, setting her hair in motion swinging about her face.

He began the careful exit down the bumpy dirt road. They drove in silence, finally exiting at the paved portion. Thibault turned right and Gemma started talking fast.

"Wait—where are you going? We need to go the other way!"

He turned to face her. "Like I said, we're going to my place to pick something up."

"Well, how far is it?"

"Less than 10 minutes."

She exhaled loudly, slouched down in the seat with her hands crossed over her chest and scowled out the windshield. She didn't make any movement until he signaled a turn onto the road by the convenience store, veering onto a side road and then the dirt path leading up to his house.

"Where are we?"

"Out in the country. This is my place."

She peered ahead at the fields of grass. Beyond a clump of trees and a quick turn in the driveway, the house appeared. She got out and stood by the truck.

"Place needs a dog," she said as she followed him up the wide steps to the porch.

"It would be a lonely hound most of the time."

"That's a nice touch," she said, noticing a rocking chair on the porch.

Thibault held the screen door open for her and unlocked the front door, then disappeared into the back of the house while she stood in the hallway. When he came back, he said, "Okay, I've got it."

She looked down at the book in his hand by a best-selling motivational speaker. She looked sideways at him.

"So, did you find it?"

"What?"

"Your purpose," she said, pointing to the title.

He laughed. "Working on it." He moved towards the door.

"Not so fast, Sergeant Steve. Don't think you'll get rid of me so soon now after luring me all the way out here. Show me around a bit." She surveyed the wide planks of the wood floors.

He began with the obvious. "Well, it's old. Not so old by Leesborough standards, but about 1860."

"This is the great room, as the real estate agents say," she said, moving into a space with a couch, big screen television mounted on one wall and bookshelves on another.

He noticed that she had spied the frog collection and he moved along so she would have to follow.

"Not so great. It's the parlor. No open plan in those days. The house was built in the old style of a central hall with four rooms coming off, one in each direction. In the summer you can open the windows and doors and get a good breeze. See," he motioned to another room, the same size as the parlor and directly behind it that looked like it functioned as a home office. The rooms were sparsely furnished in heavy Victorian furniture, upholstered in a wine-colored material.

"What's on the other side?" She had already moved in that direction.

He led her to the back of the house. "Dining room up front and kitchen behind, although originally there was a cookhouse set out in the yard. Upstairs also four rooms but I changed it around a bit. The old down here and the modern upstairs." They walked into the kitchen. "Except for the kitchen, of course. Would you like something to drink?"

"Sure, something cold." He pushed the bottles of beer aside and took out two diet sodas from the back of the refrigerator, held them up, "This okay? Glass?"

She shook her head and sat herself on a stool with her

elbows on the countertop as he handed her the can. "The furniture really goes well with the house."

"It was my grandparents' house," he said.

His cell phone pinged with a text and he looked down at it.

"Tell me, I heard there was a ruckus with Walter Benson at a party last night."

"Long, boring story."

"I'm up for a long, boring story," he said.

She said simply, "They do not like each other. Benson tried to show up Werner's research at a major academic meeting with a paper of his own this past year, so I heard. Big mistake." She shook her finger for emphasis.

"Isn't it what you call science? Challenging ideas and theories?"

She widened her eyes. "Not when you embarrass your major professor. That's what you call academic suicide."

"Is Werner so narrow-minded?"

"I wouldn't call it that, but you saw his general demeanor. He's a very proud person." She stopped to clarify. "He's just protecting his reputation. Which is formidable. He is an internationally recognized expert, you know. He's got a high profile, plenty of administration support, lots of grant money, I could go on and on. But Werner is a perfectionist; he gives you a monumental task and then he butts in and supervises every little detail himself." She paused for a gulp of soda. "I had to call the rental place three times to switch the make of car for this Dr. Pierce. Werner agonized over it like you can't believe. Too small? Too big? Too ostentatious?" She laughed, recalling the conversation.

"Micromanager?"

She nodded with a grin.

"He doesn't seem like a fun guy to work for."

"Maybe not fun, but I was lucky to have gotten this job. And even luckier to leave the toxic place where I used to work."

"Did you work in public information before?"

"No, advertising and marketing. With everything digital, the competition to be one step ahead of everyone else was getting to be so pressurized. And every day some new platform comes up and everyone scrambles to master the new shiny object. This job is more old-fashioned and civilized. It's funny," she added, "He agonizes over the details and then he'll apply for a two million dollar grant and not think twice about what he is putting down for a line-item expense. Go figure." She smiled. "He is lucky to have Beatrice around to calm him down when things get crazy. And let me tell you, we're all mighty grateful to Beatrice."

"I guess we peons all suffer the quirks of our employers. My boss gets nervous about the opinion of the politicians and the media. He doesn't need to be. He's elected and gets re-elected no matter what. That's because no one else wants his job."

"Maybe he wants to make sure no one messes with his budget. When in doubt, follow the money," she said, tapping the countertop with her finger.

He was startled to hear her use the phrase that had been rattling around in his head earlier as he pondered the Colter's financial health.

"How is Colter doing financially, by the way?"

"That's not my responsibility but from what I gather, things are good. The University subsidizes part of the Werners' salaries, the Colter family made an endowment, and although I don't write the grants, I do announce when one is secured. The place seems to be doing just fine."

"We don't have much opportunity for grants except some federal ones that require us to hire new officers with the money but then assume funding their positions in years to come. The elected folks here never want to mess with our budget because the public would scream about crime in the streets," he said.

"In Leesborough?" she laughed. "Are you kidding me? Unless I'm missing something, we aren't talking New York City here."

"We are not even talking Raleigh. But there's no logical reason for how people perceive things sometimes. All those true crime shows get people worked up." He downed the rest of his soda and crushed the can. "Ready?"

"Don't I get to see the upstairs?" she asked.

"No, too messy. There's a bathroom down here if you need it."

"No, but thanks anyway."

He held the screen door open for her and, as he closed the front door, his phone pinged again, and he looked down at it. "Just my partner getting released from the hospital."

"Was he shot?" she asked in alarm.

"That's a strange thing to ask. No, just had a medical

thing." He turned the key in the lock quickly and let the screen door slam.

They made the trip towards the Raleigh suburb where she lived quickly and in silence, conversing only to share directions to her apartment. He pulled into the parking lot, and she let herself out while the truck was still running.

"I hope you get your car taken care of," he said, for something to say. "If you need anything, just holler. You know how to holler, don't you?"

"You have no idea." She laughed and closed the truck's door. He waited until she had ascended to the second floor, stopped in front of a door, taken out her key and waved at him.

Then she moved to the window and peeked around the edge to see if he was still looking.

He was and evidently thinking of something that furrowed his brow.

Thibault drove back to Leesborough, returned the book to Gustafson's tidy desktop, then went to his own office, opened his computer and looked at the several email messages. He was too distracted. All could wait until tomorrow. He turned it off, left and drove to the supermarket to pick up a packet of fried chicken, potato salad and some apples. There was a baseball game on TV, and he could watch in his boxer shorts if he wished.

His phone rang again as he walked into the kitchen. He set the grocery sacks on the counter and saw that it was his mother calling.

"Steve, honey?"

"Hello, Momma, I just got in this minute."

"Daddy and I were wondering where you were. I wanted to call earlier but he said I shouldn't disturb you at work. How is everything?" The loaded question.

"Everything's fine, just fine." He knew she knew. But he wasn't going to say anything about it. "Oh, hey. Mutt's in the hospital. Rather, was. Emergency hemorrhoid surgery."

"Oh, bless his heart." She relayed the names of those people in her family and acquaintance who had similarly suffered, referring to them as piles, however. "You give him our best when you see him, hear?"

"Sure, Momma. You know I was supposed to go on vacation a week from now, but with Mutt in the hospital, I don't know if I'll be going then."

"That's a darn shame," she said. He heard her repeat the last part of his sentence to his father who was standing next to the phone, as usual during family calls.

"Hey, Momma, I've got to go. But I'll be dropping by on Sunday after church." He meant after she and his father were done with church. With his brother and sister-in-law away on vacation, it was just the two of them for the traditional Sunday dinner, so they would be going out to a local restaurant instead.

"Well, honey, come out to dinner with us, too."

A few okays later, he hung up. He had only put off the inevitable conversation about the breakup with his former fiancée for another day, but it worked for now. As he walked back past the living room, he saw the shelf of frogs. A detour to the kitchen to retrieve a plastic grocery sack and then back to the shelf where the lot of them was swept into the bag and the bag dumped into the kitchen trash.

After a shower, he got into shorts and a tee shirt and set up his meal on a plate on the coffee table in front of the television. The game wasn't on yet, so he watched the tail end of the news with sports and weather. No rain coming yet.

Later, after he had finished his meal and one beer, he stacked the dishes in the sink. He leafed through a magazine to distract himself from an incredibly boring and one-sided game. He looked out the window and could see the wind had picked up again, although he couldn't hear it for the hum of the overhead fan. He got up, put on shoes and left the house. He got into his truck and started to drive. Windows open, SiriusXM turned off, just a nice breeze.

He drove in through Leesborough avoiding the new areas of town and went along the main street, its sidewalks interrupted with projections of planters defining the parking areas. The street was so narrow it had been made into a one-way street several years ago. When he was a kid, you could drive right up to the front of whatever store you wanted to go to, no parking meters, no parking spaces, and stay as long as you liked. Mr. Coleman, the real estate agent, had an office right next to the drug store. Old Mr. Davis, the pharmacist, died about ten years ago and now the drug store sold just stuff: perfumed candles and stationery and things appealing to women who were always talking about what new things were to be found there when they gathered at Sunday dinners. Better than talking about who had been in Davis's pharmacy to get prescriptions for what ailment, though, he supposed.

Davis's used to sell ice cream cones in the summer. In his memory, great big ones. He and his brother would walk into town and buy one while the matrons stood uneasily at the pharmacy counter as Mr. Davis waited on the two of them. People railed against anonymity these days, but was it so bad? Twenty years ago, everybody in Leesborough knew everything about everybody else. The only relief came if you were lucky enough to go away to college or the Army. Finally, a little space.

He drove aimlessly, no one on the streets except for two kids with skateboards trying tricks on the cement curbs in front of the library. He swung around and headed back out the other way and found himself driving along a road taking him back towards Raleigh now that he knew where Gemma lived. But he thought better of it, turned on the radio to the SiriusXM country station and tried to think of nothing all the way home instead.

Chapter 7

Thibault began the next day with the resolve to get someone to help him through as many interviews as possible despite the lack of cooperation from Aileen. He had a long morning talking to five more students, only one of them male, and although they were enthusiastic about the work, the Center and Dr. Werner, none seemed to know Walter Benson well enough to give more than a physical description. He got a kick out of the workers, however, their optimism and commitment.

Taking a break, he left his jacket in Winkelman's office and walked outside toward the road, feeling good to be moving although the air was stifling and humid; there were probably no benefits to being outside except not breathing air-conditioned air. His father and mother would tell stories of what it was like before air condi-tioning and how the coldest place to go was a movie theater. No wonder it was such a popular place to be no matter what was showing. Although their home sat beneath gigantic trees whose shade cooled it sufficiently, the Thibaults, too, succumbed to air conditioning. Momma and Daddy's bedroom first, then the living room and finally the room he shared with his brother. His grandfather, whose house he now inhabited, had been appalled by the luxury and decried the Yankee influence that was the root of all evil and caused good people to go soft. No admirer of the Colters, either, Grandaddy would have been stunned by everything about the Colter Center.

The Center's setting was breathtaking, however. Edmund Colter had made an excellent choice for the property, deep in the woods and set off in what was probably a natural meadow. But Thibault thought the architecture was odd. To him the ultra-modern look of the place was jarring in that tranquil setting. For some reason, his mind went back to one of the last desultory discussions with Lallie about their relationship. He had only been half listening to what she had been saying in her calm, non-emotional way. It was many of the same themes: his inability to open up, her needs unmet, and so on, while he diligently sat across from her, listening yet not listening. He just wanted the conversation to be over and to be excused.

He shook off his thoughts and plunged across the tall grass to the upper entry. As soon as he opened the door, he could hear yelling and what sounded like objects falling. Mary stood at the top of the stairs, and he asked her, "What's going on?"

"Animal escape," she answered calmly, looking down the staircase.

Thibault walked down the steps but couldn't reach the first floor because of a long, expandable gate two workers had just put in place.

"I'd keep out of the way, if I were you," Victor Allen said as he went past on the other side of the gate, moving surprisingly nimbly for such a large man.

Thibault stood on the next to the last step and looked to his right, down the length of the corridor. Toward the end he saw a clump of people walking slowly and carefully.

He heard footsteps behind him and asked aloud, "Why doesn't the animal run down toward the other wing?"

"They put up a roadblock there just like this one," Gemma said behind him, then squeezed in front of him in order to see better.

Thibault craned his head around the corner and saw a clumsy chicken wire fence about five feet high standing on wheels that fit the width of the corridor perfectly. He asked her, "What if the monkey jumps over the roadblock?"

"It's a galago," said Ty as he descended the stairs. "Not a monkey."

"If it jumps over the roadblock, that's when the fun really begins." Gemma leaned back a little and Thibault could smell her hair.

There were orders given and then a brown animal hopped down the hall keeping close to the wall. It stopped midway, turned and looked at the pursuers: Victor Allen, Werner, Paige and one of the female workers he had interviewed earlier. Both of the women held the large nets.

"See?" Gemma said, pointing to the nets. "I wasn't making it up about the nets."

He shook his head. "Okay, I believe you now."

"Get me some gloves," Werner yelled to nobody in particular.

"Yeah, right," said Ty under his breath.

"I've got a pair here," said Beatrice Werner from behind them as she came past them down the stairs.

"Give me the net," Werner said to Paige.

"Calm down, I've got it," Paige answered, crouching low and moving closer.

Werner now directed his remarks to the worker at his side. "Give me the net."

Cowed by his imperious tone, the worker leaned the net against the corridor's wall and began to remove her gloves. As she fumbled with the gloves, the net slid down, making a screeching sound before it crashed to the ground. The animal flew off the ground and landed on the side of Bruce's cage with its hands and feet on the mesh.

"Watch out! Get him off there!" someone yelled.

Bruce screamed and clawed at the animal's hands, then leaned over to bite at the intruding digits. The brown mass flew off the cage before Paige could get near and raced down the hall, stopping suddenly when it saw the group of people behind the roadblock.

Werner yelled to the worker, "Are you the person responsible for letting the galago out of the cage in the first place?"

"Shh," Victor Allen said as he walked quietly down the hall.

Paige continued walking stealthily, almost in a crouch, ignoring the renewed screams of Bruce as she passed his cage.

"Who is responsible for this?" Werner bellowed, one gloved hand on his hip and the other grasping the net.

Allen turned on him. "Let's deal with fixing it. And give me the net," he added. He put one hand on it, and they grappled for a moment.

"I don't believe this," Thibault said. He rested his hand on Gemma's shoulder to get a better look and it was like a shock passing down her arm.

"I do," Ty said with a snigger.

Allen succeeded in pulling the net away and turned back to the animal.

"Careful, he's injured," Beatrice said. The animal was leaving bloody footprints as it moved along the floor.

'That's the trouble with these escapes," Gemma said to Thibault. "The animals freak out and get injured bashing into things. If not, they manage to bite someone, which is not a whole lot better."

Paige crept closer, her movements careful and smooth. With her eyes still on the animal, she said in a low voice, "Is the box ready?"

Thibault looked over and saw a small wooden cage with wire windows the worker had brought forward.

"Just keep it ready," Paige said. "Don't put the roadblock down until he's secure in the net. When he's in the net, come through with the box and put the roadblock back up."

"She's really good," Ty said. "Diana, the huntress."

Victor Allen had progressed only as far as Bruce's cage when the animal screamed. He pulled himself back quickly. "We have got to do something about that blasted animal." He and Werner moved purposefully down the hall at a rapid pace but stopped about ten feet behind Paige.

"Come on now, Sammy," Paige said to the animal as she inched closer. The galago just stared but sat up on its back legs. Then it slowly flattened out its ears and parted its lips in a wide, humorless smile.

"Come on now. You want lunch, don't you?" she continued.

The animal kept looking at her but leaned forward slightly. Paige started to put her net down towards the wall on her right, leaving a large open space to her left. The animal leaned forward a bit more.

"Come on, Sammy." Just as the animal began its leap, Paige arced the net in the air and down quickly to her left as the animal jumped into it. She turned the net face down on the ground and stood on the metal handle to prevent further escape. But the animal was not trying to get out of the net, he was on his hind legs again, ears back, teeth bared, vocalizing in anger.

"Bravo, Paige," Beatrice said loudly as clapping broke out.

"Years of tennis really paid off," Ty said.

Werner and Allen ran down the hall. Allen put his thumb and forefinger around the back of Sammy's neck, immobilizing a potential bite while Paige disentangled the net from its hands and feet. In a few moments, the animal was dropped in the box, locked in and hauled off to the sick bay for treatment.

"That was easy," Thibault said, removing his hand from Gemma's shoulder. The roadblocks came down and were taken back to the maintenance room, the workers went back down the hall, the excitement was over.

Thibault looked around for Beatrice, but she had disappeared. Well, he'd get to her later. At least he knew she was probably no longer ill. He caught up to Gemma at the head of the stairs.

"How's the car?" he asked.

"They gave me a loaner. They actually brought it to my place. I couldn't believe it!"

He looked at her quizzically. "Why?"

"Back home you have to beg to get a loaner. And delivered? No way!" She looked at her watch. "It's after one already and I haven't had lunch. Is your offer still good from yesterday?"

He paused a moment.

"About lunch?" she prompted.

"Sure," he said, shaking his head. "We Southerners are sometimes a little slow on the uptake."

"I noticed," she said. But she smiled when she said it.

Chapter 8

"What a day," Gemma said as they bumped along the dirt road on their way out of the Center. The dust of the road rose in orange-red clouds and coated the side windows and obscured vision to the back. The bushes on the side of the road were likewise coated in dust.

Gemma adjusted a vent to blow the car's air conditioning directly at her face. She pulled her hair back and held it on top of her head, exposing the damp strands clinging to her neck. Thibault noticed a mole just above her collarbone.

"I must have had fifty phone calls this morning—administration, department, press. We made the evening news last night and the papers this morning. And of course, it's all over the internet."

Thibault's eyes were fixed on the road as he paid attention to dodging the next rut. "I try to keep away from internet news if I can help it. Too many clickbait stories about a celebrity's 'heartbreaking' loss that turns out to be missing out on a role."

"The coverage was pretty straight forward, except the spin makes it seem like some accident." She looked over at him. "That's a blessing for now. It could have been very sensationalistic."

Thibault leaned forward to get a better view of the track ahead.

"It's surprising how dense the forest is here, it's so dark you could almost think it was evening in some places," she said.

"I hadn't been out on this particular road before the incident," Thibault said. "I can tell you most locals won't venture out here."

"Because of the crappy roads?" Gemma laughed.

"No, because several people have died in these woods over the years." He looked at her to indicate he was not just trying to scare her. "It's got a dark reputation, that's all. If Edmund Colter had spent more time actually living around here, he would never have chosen this location for his Center."

Her eyes widened, nonetheless. "I don't want to hear those kinds of stories, thank you. I scare easily."

They soon came out to the paved road, and he turned the truck left, which took them in a direction opposite from the main road. Some minutes later they were at the outskirts of Leesborough and parked in front of Loretta's B-B-Q, a converted double wide trailer with an aluminum awning hanging over wooden steps and a screen door.

Loretta herself greeted them as they stood with their trays in front of the steam tables. "Well, hello, stranger," she said in a loud voice over the banging of another server's big metal spoon on the counter.

"Hey." Thibault nodded with a slight smile.

"What you want?" she asked.

Although they were at the tail end of lunchtime for most people here, there were still plenty of choices. "I recommend the pork barbeque," Thibault said to Gemma and ordered some for himself.

She hesitated, looking at the other choices in front of her, which seemed to be fried chicken, some kind of meat patties, steamed greens, okra, mashed potatoes and sweet potatoes.

"You've lived here how long?" he said, wondering why she looked puzzled at the choices. Without waiting for an answer, he ordered for them both.

Loretta took a white hamburger bun out of a plastic bag and spooned light-colored chopped meat onto it. "Slaw?" Thibault nodded and she put a large spoonful onto the meat. "Greens?" He nodded again and she set the plate on top of glass counter and prepared another plate. "Tea with extra lemon, right?" He nodded again and Gemma agreed.

"And a slice of peach pie?" The other server rang them up at the end of the counter and they moved into the other part of the trailer where picnic tables and chairs were located.

"When you really want to impress a woman—especially not a local—you bring them to Loretta's and you always order the barbecue," Thibault said.

"Do you always do that switching?" she asked as they sat at the backmost table overlooking a small clearing.

Thibault didn't answer.

"You know, Standard English and then, um, Southern English?"

He still didn't answer.

"What part of what I said didn't you understand?" she continued quickly, laughing.

"Oh, I understood your question, all right. I'm just without a proper answer, that's all."

Gemma shrugged. "Don't mind me. I tend to be direct." She took a bite of the sandwich, her eyes growing wide. "This is good! But why is it called barbecue if there isn't barbecue sauce on it?"

Thibault was thinking of the many ways to respond to this, with a real explanation, with a pretense of shock, with condescension, with a joke, but she was already on to the next topic.

"How are things going so far?"

"I'll have some information from the autopsy soon."

She shuddered. "Have you talked to many people yet?"

He swallowed a bite of his sandwich and deliberated about answering. "The janitor, Dr. Allen, Ty and Paige. And some of the girls who work for Dr. Allen."

"What did you think?"

"Of the young girls?"

She paused and gave him a look.

He tried again. "Oh, you mean the barbecue. The slaw? Both excellent today."

She opened her eyes wide and stated, "I get it. You enjoy playing deliberately dense, Sergeant Steve."

He paused for as long as he thought she could stand it. "I prefer the word 'obtuse' a little more. And yes, it's often an effective strategy."

She laughed. "Let me begin again: what did you think of what people had to tell you?" She looked intently at him.

He busied himself putting sugar into his iced tea.

"Why are you doing that? They have sweet tea here. I saw it written on the board out there."

"Proportions are not right," he said and then added, "You're awfully opinionated."

She laughed and resumed eating.

He said in an official tone, "Did it occur to you a murder investigation is serious, and the information is confidential?" He could see her straighten up as if to retort and then change her tack.

"Look, I'm in public relations. I can't help myself. Information is everything. The more I can control what to feed the media, the better off we'll be. If we keep quiet, it's just destructive. We don't want to make it seem like some dark mystery is being covered up."

"I can see your point," he said, wiping his mouth with a napkin. "You can tell him things are moving along at a fair pace. You know, moving along at a goodly pace."

"Tell who?"

"Werner. Isn't that why you're asking?"

She rolled her eyes. "No. And there you go again. Switching. But thanks for translating this time."

She opened the bun on her plate and started eating the pork and the slaw with a fork. "You know, aside from its being my job, I believe in the Center and what it's doing. It might not be finding a cure for cancer, but the research is valuable, and it doesn't harm the animals and really should continue. We don't want this isolated incident to affect all the work going on."

"I certainly hope it is isolated."

"You never know where new discoveries can come from. Who could have guessed when Columbus sailed off to find a route to the East Indies, he would set such a chain of events into motion?"

"Annihilation of Native American tribes, venereal diseases, enslavement…"

"Okay, okay. Lots of bad stuff. But from a personal standpoint, I'd rather be where I am today than in some small Italian village like my grandparents, trying to eke a living out of bare rock."

"Nothin' worse than eking," Thibault said.

"You're impossible," she said with a smile. "Where is your family from?"

"The Thibaults are from Charleston originally. French Huguenots with a small shipping company. The War, the Civil War is what we mean when we say, 'The War,' wiped them out financially, so my one-legged ancestor moved his family to near Raleigh, where his wife's family had land. They took a step down in life and grew tobacco."

"Did they have slaves?"

"They were too poor."

"Oh," her face colored a bit, but she was without words for only a few moments. "Where I'm from in suburban New Jersey everything still feels so new. Of course, there are the families that have been there for generations, but for the most part people are known for their mobility. I'm second generation, a relative old-timer by some standards." She leaned forward, hands supporting her face, and she slowed her talking down for once. "What's it like to have such deep roots in a place?"

He tilted back in his chair and answered slowly. "I couldn't really say. I don't know any other life. Some people would find it stifling, I suppose. But the good side is you're accepted for what you are, no matter what it is." He looked out the window at a rabbit running from the shade of one pine sapling to another. "Most of the time."

He looked back at her. "No, it's bullshit, actually, if you'll excuse my language. Sometimes it's insufferable, and I couldn't think of anything more appealing than getting a job somewhere like California and starting over."

"And your farm?"

"Well, as I said, *sometimes* the thought is appealing."

She pushed her plate to the side. "That's what I did. I just packed up and moved here. Didn't know a soul."

"I admire that," he said. "I went to UNC and got my master's at the University, so I never really left the area. But it would feel funny going somewhere entirely new and trying to pass myself off as someone I'm not."

"No, no, that's not it. You decide who you're going to be, and you become it. It's not like pretending to be rich or having a degree you didn't earn. You decide to be something, a goal setter or a non-victim, take your choice, and then you do it. And pretty soon you are it. It *is* you."

"Just create who you want to be?"

"Exactly. Fake it until you make it."

He looked out the window past his reflection. "Sounds interesting—but maybe I am too utterly conventional." He smiled.

"Nah, I don't think so. Give it a shot."

Thibault didn't know why he had said it because he knew he was not utterly conventional, and it was one of the issues Lallie had with him. She humored him about restoring his grandparents' farmhouse, but there was no way she was going to live there. That was what upscale housing developments were for. He also knew it had been a risk to take Gemma out to Loretta's for lunch. Not from his work perspective, but because someone was likely to have seen him and he'd hear about it come Sunday.

"You seem to have veered off the subject of quizzing me about what I know. I'm afraid you're going to get in trouble with Dr. Werner," he said.

"I feel like I'm always on the brink of getting into trouble with him. It has been the strangest working relationship I've ever had." She made a wry face.

"What's Dr. Allen's relationship with Werner all about?"

She rolled her eyes. "Off the record, all right?"

He laughed. "You keep talking to me like I'm a reporter. I'm a cop and everything is on the record with me, but obviously not going to be published anywhere."

She pondered this a moment but continued. "See, from what I've heard, Werner helped Allen get the job. Strictly hearsay, because obviously I wasn't here then, but I heard he had an interesting history with female students, which led to his leaving his former position at Michigan. Werner helped get him hired here."

"How's that?"

"Werner's on the Board of the Colter Foundation."

"Aha," Thibault said.

"And despite any personal faults, Allen is a good academic, veterinarian and administrator. Werner even ignored Beatrice's advice on the hire, so I'm told. It had to be a first. She supports him in everything he does and tries to stay in the background."

"Has he ever hit on you?"

"Werner?" she asked incredulously.

"No, Victor Allen."

"Oh, of course. Week one. The man has a voracious libido. His theory, which he was charming enough to share with me, is that someone is bound to say yes sooner or later. Whether out of attraction, boredom, revenge, a sense of danger or too much alcohol, he doesn't seem to care."

"I had a roommate with the same theory." Thibault said. "It was a surprisingly successful approach. If you're not particular."

"Anyway, Werner got him the director's job and Allen started flexing his muscles a little bit more than Werner liked. It's a bit of push and pull all the time, but I manage to stay out of the crossfire."

"You just keep the adjoining door to your office closed."

"Yep."

Thibault stood up and helped her with her chair, to her surprise.

"We've spent this entire lunch with you worming information out of me, not the other way around," she accused him good naturedly.

"That's why I'm a cop and you're in public relations."

Chapter 9

Thibault dropped Gemma back at the Primate Center, went in and made his way to the wing where Benson's body had been found. He walked inside quietly, careful not to disturb the animals or interfere with anyone observing them up above. He looked through the window of the door on Z's cage, but she was evidently outside. He walked over to the net hung in the corner of the wing and lifted it up. The pole, fairly light, was made of aluminum and likely not used to hit Walter Benson. If it had been, it would have had a significant dent in it and certainly would not have inflicted a fatal injury. He turned it around in his hands. If Walter were hit. Maybe Walter was pushed down and hit his head on the cement underneath the sawdust. Maybe Walter had a blackout and fell and hit his head. He replaced the net and headed back outside to his truck to return to his office.

His phone rang and he pulled to the side of the road to answer.

"A Dr. Benson called," Aileen said. "Shall I text you the number?"

"No, I'm on my way back right now." It must be Walter's father.

He was just settling down in his office when Aileen's voice came through on the intercom.

"Benson on line eight."

Thibault stared at the phone. His landline calls were infrequent.

He picked up the receiver, pressed line eight and said, "Sergeant Thibault here."

"Hello. This is Dr. Edward Benson. Walter Benson's father." It was a calm voice, soft around the edges. "My wife and I are in town, and we were wondering if we could meet with you tomorrow to talk. To get more information about what exactly happened."

"First, let me say how sorry I am about your son. But I haven't talked to the Medical Examiner yet, so I don't have much information to share."

"Yes, we know. We went in this morning to do a formal identification, so we know it's early. You may not be able to draw any definite conclusions at this time, but I'd like you to know we are willing to help in any way. To provide you with any support or help."

Thibault thanked him. Then he added, "Again, I'm sorry for your loss."

"In some ways, we weren't all that surprised," Dr. Benson replied.

Thibault was stunned. What kind of parents wouldn't be surprised?

As if his silence made Dr. Benson realize how his remark must have sounded, he quickly modified it. "I meant to say, there were circumstances, not as if we were expecting this, but in a way, please, I'll explain. Are you available for lunch at the Wannamaker tomorrow?"

Thibault hesitated as he tried to think of an excuse, but Dr. Benson was decisive and quick. "Let's say one o'clock?"

Thibault assented with internal misgivings as they concluded the conversation. He then drove into Raleigh to the Medical Examiner's office, in a relatively new building several blocks away from the police department, where it had previously been squeezed into the basement. Over the years the growing department and more sophisticated equipment of the ME necessitated more space. Autopsies and their reports were processed more quickly under the new arrangement because of the separation, too, since the staff was not constantly being interrupted to provide updates. Although Leesborough had two techs in its department, they relied on Raleigh for more sophisticated assistance and autopsies, of course, not having their own Medical Examiner.

Conroy was dressed in hospital greens with a white apron over them, his hair covered with a cap, safety glasses in place, mask over his nose and mouth and gloves on his hands. He was hunched over the body of Walter Benson and speaking aloud from time to time into the microphone over the table. He caught sight of the movement of Thibault out of the corner of his eye, reached up to turn off the microphone and beckoned him into the room.

"Hey," he said cheerfully.

"Hey. Just checking up on things," Thibault said as he came through the swinging doors. The body was open from the pubic bone to the neck. Thibault stood a polite distance away.

"Parents were here this morning."

"I heard."

"I'm just putting him back together for the funeral home to pick up later."

"When's Foster coming back from vacation?"

"Next week."

"I'm getting my vacation week after this. Off to the coast."

"Don't count on it," Conroy said, stitching the skin quickly.

Thibault looked away. "You did the head already?"

"Fracture of the temporal bone, crushed. Blunt force trauma. Something wooden, there are a couple of tiny splinters, or so it seems. Broom handle, baseball bat?

"Could he have had a blackout or seizure and hit his head?"

"Well, yes, he could have, but that's kind of an odd place to land on your head. Looks like somebody clocked him." He picked up his hand and demonstrated a swing.

"Left-handed or right-handed?"

"Come on, Thibault. Don't get all Sherlock Holmes on me. Right-handed forehand or left-handed backhand. Same thing."

"I didn't notice any defense injuries on the hands."

"My, aren't we observant," Conroy remarked. "However, there is a bruise on the forearm. Could be a defense wound or maybe just when he fell." He finished up the last of the stitching. "Now, I know this fellow couldn't have been the brightest bulb because he walked into a cage with an 800-pound gorilla—."

"Hundred-and-fifty-pound chimp," Thibault corrected.

"Figure of speech." Conroy took off his mask and then his gloves. "Hmm. I've got to get something to eat."

He led the way through the double doors to the food machines in the hall a few steps outside the autopsy room. They sat in molded plastic chairs in the hall while Conroy sipped chocolate milk out of a little carton. He wiped a non-existent bit off his chin and wiped his hand on his apron next to a dark yellow stain and some dried blood. He unwrapped peanut butter cheese crackers, held the package up as an offer to Thibault, who shook his head, and resumed. "Anyway, judging by the lividity, this guy ended up face down."

"Yes and no. He was found face down, drug out, turned over and replaced face down."

"What? Well, that would explain why there was so much sawdust up his nose, I guess."

"You think maybe he was alive and inhaled it?"

"Might could. But it was really in the lower nostrils, not any higher up."

"Anything else interesting?"

"No tissue or hair under the nails, just dirt. And sawdust." He paused to put the last cracker in his mouth.

Thibault stood up. "Okay, then. Thanks. I guess I'll see the final report when I see it."

"That's right," Conroy said. "See you when I see you."

Thibault was back in his office thirty minutes later sorting through his emails when Aileen passed his door. She threw over her shoulder, "Chief wants to see you."

"What? I thought he was on vacation until next week?" he yelled to her retreating figure.

"Excuse me," she said to the hall in front of her as she continued to walk away. "Acting Chief." Her heels clicked away down the hall and shortly thereafter he could hear her footsteps coming back his way.

As she appeared in the doorway, he said, "Anybody know how Mutt is doing today?"

"I don't know. Am I supposed to be Miss Congeniality?" She stood there as he continued to sort through the message slips of calls that had come through the main line. He felt her glare on him. She was very good at glaring.

"Okay, okay, I'm coming."

She preceded him down the hall and sat herself at the desk outside Gustafson's office. Thibault knocked on the doorframe of the open door.

"Come in. Steve! How are you?" He stood and they shook hands. When Gustafson was not Acting Chief, he was not so formal.

"Tell me about the Colter thing." He motioned for Thibault to sit.

"I just talked to Conroy, and I've been talking to a whole lot of people out there. You know Mutt just got out of the hospital, so I've been working this myself so far. I could really use some help."

Gustafson lowered his voice as if someone might be listening. "I've been asked to take you off the investigation."

A moment of affront passed through him, to be replaced by a pleasant idea of being relieved of the task. Thibault held up his hands. "That's fine with me. Lord knows we are all overloaded." He wasn't thinking about how burdened they were; however, he was thinking of being free to take his vacation. Ten days from now he could be in Westport with early morning fishing and evening meals at Nemo's.

"But I am not going to take you off the case, and that's what I told them."

The smile vanished from Thibault's face. "Them?"

"Conference call from some administrator types at the University. Get this—they requested Murphy by name."

"What? Murphy is great but he's their ex-football star. Are they hoping for a quick conclusion and no bad press for them and Colter?"

"Probably. But don't worry, you're eminently qualified for this and you are the only detective we have with an advanced degree. It ought to mean something to them."

"I should say so. And it's from their University, too." Thibault was sounding indignant.

"Exactly. I said I thought you would handle the investigation with the finesse and sensitivity it deserved." Gustafson smiled.

"Sensitive guy all right, that's me."

"An important quality people often overlook. In fact, this young man's parents are in town and I've let them know you would be available to talk with them, not just an interview, but to give it to them straight. I know I should handle it, but under the circumstances—."

Thibault did not reveal he had already made a date for the next day. He hesitated for a moment and then said, "But I really need some help interviewing the work crew out there." Gustafson started to squirm in disagreement.

Thibault continued, "Otherwise, I simply won't have time to meet with the Bensons at all. Have Murphy help me, and everyone will be happy."

"All right, he can help you on a limited basis. It should satisfy everyone. We'll find out what he can put aside for the moment." He had a peeved look on his face. "Why is everyone either sick or on vacation?" He caught himself and got up to indicate the conversation was over.

Thibault got up swiftly before anything else was thrown his way. They shook hands again. Thibault stopped at the doorway and added, "Oh, and thanks for the book."

"Did you like it?"

"It was really interesting," he answered.

Gustafson leaned back against his desk and was about to ask him more questions when Aileen interrupted on the intercom.

"Channel 10 news reporter on line five. Do you want to take it?"

Gustafson made a face and before he could sit down and take the call, Thibault was already halfway down the hall.

Chapter 10

Thibault took off his jacket and tie and plunged back into his hot truck. He turned on the air conditioning and opened the windows to push the stale air out and drove over to Walter Benson's apartment on the edge of Raleigh. Typically, it was a place two-career newlyweds lived who liked the New South architectural style. It was everywhere now, the grayish blue wood siding and wide sloping roofs. All the new vacation homes in Westport looked like this now, except for his family's old place, as did whole developments and even strip shopping centers. At least they hadn't scraped the ground entirely when they built this two-story apartment structure, leaving scattered mature trees to provide shade. Benson's apartment was on the ground floor in a group towards the far end.

Thibault slipped on gloves and put the key they had retrieved from Benson's pocket in the lock. It felt like the air conditioning had been turned down, either to save money or because Benson knew he would not be back for many hours. In any case, the room was warmer than was comfortable and smelled of clothes and stale cigarette smoke. He walked straight ahead to the sliding glass doors and drew the curtains open halfway for some light. Behind him was a gray couch looking like part of the five-piece suites advertised in local furniture rental ads. The coffee table was pressed wood with a plastic veneer with books and papers strewn on top and onto the floor. The couch and table faced a widescreen television. He took quick photos with his phone for his own reference; the techs might be called in to do a more thorough job.

Thibault moved to the dining area that looked like it was seldom used except to receive piles of sorted mail and bills. He went into the kitchen, a long, windowless alcove with a countertop bar facing the living room. He turned on the light and looked at the dirty dishes soaking in water and a dead cockroach floating on top. He looked in the refrigerator: a couple of beers, lunch meat, milk, condiments, some frozen dinners in the freezer.

Off the living room was a closet with several coats, jackets and cartons of papers. Down the hall he poked around in the bathroom, noting in the medicine cabinet plastic prescription bottles prescribed by Dr. E. Benson. He rearranged them with the labels facing out and took another picture. The bedrooms were further down the short hall, and one contained an unmade bed, clothes on the floor, books on the night table and on the floor next to the bed. The other bedroom was the same size and Thibault guessed this might have been Ty's room when he lived here. It was now a sparsely furnished study with two laminate bookshelves and a small desk with a laptop and a printer on top.

He sat down in what looked like one of the chairs from the dining area and clicked the mouse and saw that it the laptop hadn't been turned off, again indicating that Benson had expected to return. There was nothing noted on the Google calendar and clicking back through the past month Thibault could see Benson had probably never used it. He went back and clicked on contacts and saw a substantial list.

He went back to the dock at the bottom of the screen and clicked on the Word program. The directory didn't contain many files, which surprised him, the earliest dating back to a few weeks ago. He clicked on each file in turn. Several were a series of incomplete sentences looking like notes or ideas to pursue. The rest of the files were papers dealing with animal behavior, less than a dozen pages long with a statistical portion included. At the end of it there was a brief bio. It looked like something he planned to submit to a journal rather than for classwork. But the other papers appeared to be work submitted for various classes.

Where was the rest of Benson's work? Was there another computer somewhere? Or was everything on thumb drives?

He opened the desk drawer and sifted through loose ATM receipts, paper clips and Post-it notes. From the back of the drawer, he pulled out an appointment book. Thibault flipped through it and found names listed for almost every day, including weekends, back to January and ahead a few weeks from now. Sandy, Red T., Blanche. It looked like quite a social life. But there were no appointments listed for this week with any of the people he knew to be associated with Colter unless these were all nicknames or aliases. He was going to have to find someone to help him cross-reference these with the names of everyone who worked or visited out there. Under the calendar in the drawer was a small key, like the kind for a file cabinet. Thibault looked around and did not see a file cabinet. He looked in the closet of the room and then looked in the bedroom's closet. He saw a beige file cabinet with a key in the lock. He took it out and tried the key he had in his hand, but it didn't fit.

While he stood there, he heard a door open and close, and footsteps move into the tiled dining area. The air conditioning kicked on. He walked quietly down the hall and stood in the doorway while a woman, backlit from the sliding doors was sorting through the mail on the coffee table.

"Can I help you with something?" he asked.

Paige gasped, put her hand to her chest and said, "Oh, Sergeant Thibault. You gave me such a fright!" She moved a piece of hair that had fallen into her face. "I was just checking on things.

Thibault came closer. "How did you get in?" he asked, sure that he hadn't left it unlocked.

"I have a key. Ty's key," she answered quickly. She looked down at his gloved hands. "Oh. I'm sorry. I thought it would be all right to come in. Walter's parents asked me to pick up a few things."

"Any thumb drives for example?"

She allowed herself a sad smile. "No, they asked me to get his things organized. So it wouldn't be so painful for them. You understand."

"Yes," he said, watching her eyes survey the room quickly.

"Despite their wishes, I don't want you to move anything just yet." He stood facing her and watched her quick eyes at work scanning the room. "There is something you could help me with, though." She looked interested at the suggestion.

Thibault led the way back to Benson's study. He opened the closet door and turned to look at Paige. Her eyes, which had been busy surveying the room, focused attention on the beige file cabinet.

"Now, I'm a bit puzzled," Thibault began. "I've looked in the computer and there don't seem to be as many files as you might expect from such an industrious person as Walter Benson."

"Well, he'd only been here a year, after all." She considered a moment and asked, "What files are you looking for exactly?"

"Term papers, research papers, that sort of thing. And there is nothing too old in there, either. Nothing from before he got here, it looks like."

"Oh." She had crossed her arms over her chest and was looking beyond him into the closet. "A lot of people don't bother to save outdated papers. And maybe he bought this computer new when he got here and didn't transfer anything onto it."

She smiled at the convenient explanation.

He turned and opened the top drawer of the file cabinet. "You'd think he might have kept a hard copy." As he talked, he flipped through files containing the apartment's lease, car insurance documents, course outlines, and a large folder with travel articles cut from newspapers and magazines. He opened the second drawer.

"Aha!" Thibault said.

Paige, who had been looking over his shoulder, moved in closer. They both looked at files of papers Benson had written, neatly filed by subject and then by date. There were about twenty-five papers here—many more than there were in the computer, although some were written during the same period. Thibault opened the first manila file and flipped through it.

"What are you looking for? Exactly?"

"I want to know where the digital copy is."

Paige offered, "Maybe they are on thumb drives. Or he erased them because they were no longer of any use and took up too much space."

"That seems unlikely. Maybe someone else erased them," he countered. He replaced the file folders in the cabinet. "I would just expect—."

He pushed the drawer in, and it came off its roller slightly. He knelt down and jiggled it and then pulled it out to reposition it. "Well, would you look at this!" he exclaimed. Paige moved in closer to look. He reached his hand to the back of the drawer and said, "What do you think I found?"

She managed a smile. "I can't imagine."

"A three-hole punch!" He held it aloft in front her face. "These are pretty darned hard to find, let me tell you. I bet he had been looking for this thing for months," Thibault said. He watched as annoyance and relief flicked across Paige's face.

He realigned the file drawer, replaced it and stood up.

"I guess there aren't any more copies of his papers then," she stated.

"Nope, other than what's in the cabinet. Unless, of course, he stored them somewhere else." Thibault smiled, fingering the key in his pocket he had no intention of bringing out.

He looked at his watch since he wanted to see Mutt soon.

"Better be going," he announced as he turned off the light and went back through the apartment to the living room. He closed the drapes on the sliding glass door, making sure it was locked first. He walked over to the dining area and saw the thermostat at eye level and adjusted the temperature up to seventy-eight degrees. She had moved it down to seventy-two when she came in, probably planning on staying for a while.

He moved towards the front door and held out his hand. "And you'd better let me have that key. I'll give it to the Bensons."

She took it out of her purse and slowly handed it to him. She stood a moment as if expecting him to say something. So, he did.

"Good day."

Thibault drove towards Mutt's house wondering what Paige had been searching for. He didn't trust her and chuckled at being able to goad her so easily, although it was Mutt who was an expert at flustering people when he wanted to. What a time for him to be incapacitated.

Mae answered the door looking stressed as well as peeved. He gave her a hug.

"Bad patient?" he asked.

"Don't get me started," she replied.

Mutt looked terrible. He was propped up in bed dressed in pajama bottoms and a white tee shirt that drained the color from his dark brown face. He was looking at a large screen television, mounted over the chest of drawers, that played some movie but the sound had been turned down.

"Hey," Thibault said softly as he walked up to the bed.

Mutt blinked his eyes and smiled broadly. "Hey, T," he replied, struggling to sit up more.

"Whoa," Thibault cautioned. "Nice vacation you picked out for yourself. Me, I'll be lucky to get any time off now that you're laid up."

"Sorry about that. Here, just help me up here, and I'm ready to get back to work," he said, handing Thibault the remote and bluffing an attempt to get out of bed.

Thibault laughed and pulled a chair up to the bed. "I didn't get you a card or a box of candy. Nothing." Mutt dismissed this with a wave of his hand. "I just ain't had the time today. And yesterday Mae said you weren't fit to talk to anybody."

Mutt said nothing.

"Now me, I've been out interviewing all day yesterday and today, and then I had to go talk to Gustafson."

Mutt started to laugh and then grimaced in pain.

"How soon will you be up and about?" Thibault asked.

"Hey, don't push it. Of all the humiliation, I have to sit on this stupid-ass rubber doughnut, too." He shook his head. "And then I will have to put up with all the jokes when I get back."

Thibault said, "You know I will do my best not to partake in any jocular comments."

"Sure, sure." Mutt pursed his lips and looked towards the windows where the light was finally starting to fade.

Thibault began, "So listen. I want to run this thing by you." Mutt rubbed the palms of his huge hands over his eyes and onto his temples as if to clear his head.

Thibault thought better of getting into too much detail since Mutt didn't seem to be focusing all too well; his summary of the events and aftermath at Colter was quite brief. "My preferred theory is the chimp was trained to do it. Even though I came up with it myself, it is pretty far-fetched."

"Murders in the Rue Morgue?" Mutt asked.

Thibault laughed. "Yeah, that's right. I always liked that story. This guy Benson evidently wasn't likeable and insulted his boss—about what, I haven't got a clear picture yet—but they had a brief history of causing each other grief. Then again, Aileen's been doing it to all of us for years and no one has killed her yet."

"Yet."

"The poor guy got whacked on the head, he didn't seem to ward off the blow, like he didn't know it was coming, or it was someone he knew, or—."

"He didn't know it was coming. Who do you think?" Mutt asked.

"Too many possibilities just now and not enough information."

Mutt said nothing for a full minute. "T, you've got your hands full," he said in a voice sounding tired. "How are you holding up?"

Thibault looked at Mutt carefully. Was he talking about the job or Lallie? Hell, he probably knew about that, too. He stood up. "I'd better let you catch up on your movie." He patted Mutt on the arm. "I'll check in tomorrow to see how things are going." Mutt had closed his eyes, but he smiled.

As he walked to his truck, Thibault inhaled the scents of the late spring flowers that Mae had planted. It made him think he ought to buy a barrel or something rustic looking and plant flowers in it in front of his porch. He'd look carefully in the next few weeks as he drove by people's homes to see what they planted here. He stopped short. Lallie had been after him to do just that for two years and he couldn't be bothered. Now that they were no longer together, he had the urge to do it.

Was he just being contrary? He loosened his tie and wondered if he really was a stubborn son of a bitch after all. No, no, he corrected himself. He was an unfeeling, stubborn son of a bitch she had said in a rare moment of strong language. Maybe he was. Or maybe he just couldn't feel the way she wanted him to, that's all.

Thibault allowed himself a sigh and, while inhaling, picked up the scent of jasmine in the air. His thoughts immediately wafted elsewhere, so he took his jacket off, got into his truck and drove all the way home with the windows rolled down.

Chapter 11

By the time he arrived at the office the next morning the autopsy report was on his desk, hand-delivered a half hour earlier. No surprises or changes from what Conroy had told him earlier except time of death was narrowed from midnight to two a.m. He picked up his cell.

"Hey, thanks for the quick turnaround. But let me ask you something: Is it possible he was not struck there in the room but somewhere else and was then drug into the room?"

"Sure, anything's possible."

"Can our techs get his clothes to see if they can pick anything up from them?"

Thibault next called the Leesborough techs. Amy answered the phone, and he asked her to drive over to Raleigh.

"I was wondering: You got any results from the stick with the key attached we got from Colter on Monday?"

"Just dirt and animal hair," she responded.

Thibault muttered to himself and then added, "Conroy's got the deceased's clothing. If you could check it for anything to indicate if the body was pulled over dirt or gravel from some other location, it would be helpful."

"Okay," she answered with a bit of doubt in her voice.

By the time Thibault had finished returning the calls from the previous day and scheduling appointments for the next two days, it was ten-thirty. He had an interview with Klaus Werner at eleven and then another one with Beatrice Werner, who had proved much more difficult to pin down. At least Gustafson had lent him two people who could assist with the student worker interviews so he could complete the first round. He could also use them to talk to Benson's neighbors at the apartment complex to ascertain who had been coming and going there over the past weeks and months, although the anonymous nature of the place might not yield anything.

He packed a briefcase with notepads and pens and made his way to the parking lot, dreading the drive to Colter, which was surely ruining his shocks and his piece of mind remembering the rumors of previous mysterious deaths in that forest. Walter Benson could now be added to the list. There better not be any more.

Thibault went in through the service entrance doors to avoid making a more public entrance. But before he went up the stairs, he detoured towards the wing where Benson had been found. He saw Bruce's cage and thought if he walked on the other side of the hall, very slowly and calmly, the animal would certainly ignore him. Not a chance. As soon as he was within one yard of the cage, Bruce lunged at the wire mesh and screamed at him.

I've got to remember not to come this way, Thibault thought to himself as he resumed a faster pace down the hall. He opened the door to the wing and saw the animal control gloves hanging next to Z's cage and the empty hook where the key stick had been removed. He heard a noise and turned quickly. The janitor, Henry Simmons, was standing almost behind the door to the wing, broom in hand, with a startled look on his face. They stared at each other for a moment.

"Anything happening with Z yet?"

"No, sir." Simmons answered.

"Sorry, I didn't mean to startle you. But you just about scared the bejeezus out of me," he laughed. "We'll get the key back to you, probably tomorrow."

"It's okay. I have a key on my ring here, and they're not going to wash down the inside cages until tomorrow anyway."

"Is it the only time they go in the cages?"

"Yes, once a week to wash them down."

"Do the workers go in the cages during feeding time?"

"The animals usually get fed outside in the good weather. Easier to clean up. You should see the mess they make when they get fed inside." He shook his head. "I'm glad I don't have to clean that up."

Thibault just grunted in reply and went out to take the elevator to the second floor. As he came out, he could hear Werner's voice booming, "What do you think I am paying you for?"

"Now, just a minute," Gemma responded firmly. Her door to the hall was open.

"Please, please." It was another woman's voice, perhaps Beatrice Werner pleading with her husband. The adjoining door was slammed, and he could hear more muffled voices through it as he stood in the hall. He saw Gemma's face in profile and the jaw muscles clenching and relaxing in a steady rhythm. He cleared his throat to get her attention, and her reddened face turned towards him. No weeping or sulking for this woman. She would probably let you have it right between the eyes.

"Everyone's gone berserk. Let's get out of here," she said tugging on his arm and propelling him towards the elevator. She punched the down button hard, crossed her arms and slouched against the back wall.

"Come on," she said, leading him towards a far wing when they reached the ground floor. She pushed open a door to the outside and showed him an observation bench in the shadow of a big pine. "No one can see you from the corridor, either upstairs or down," she said with a curt smile, plopping herself down and stretching her legs out in front of her. It was obvious this was her special break spot. He remained standing, put his hands in his pockets and jingled keys and change. The monkeys in the outside cage were barely distracted from their intense interest in the food bin.

"What was that all about?" Thibault asked.

"Some moron from one of the television stations called Werner, and proceeded to ask him if someone had been strangled by a gorilla."

Thibault said nothing. He rocked on his heels as he looked at the monkeys and rubbed the bridge of his nose.

"Well, for God's sake, it's not my job to figure out who is going to call with an inane question. Though how he got Werner's cell number is a mystery."

"Isn't anyone in the University President's office handling any of the press? Don't they have a liaison or something?"

She exhaled and ran her fingers through her hair. "The person is out on sick leave. Of course. And her assistant doesn't seem to know squat. Besides, I don't think the administration knows quite what to do about this. It's been a nightmare for me because Klaus is biting off everyone's head. Beatrice, normally a rock, has gone to pieces."

"Think how it must be for the Bensons."

She paused. "I'm sorry. I didn't mean to sound callous and self-centered. It's hard to believe this is happening. Yet Werner acts like we should all be soldiering on."

While Thibault could understand her need to talk things out, an overcast, oppressively hot day was hardly the time to be outside doing it; he was trying to think of a way to maneuver Gemma somewhere cool, like inside, and he would be happy to continue to listen. He jingled the keys in his pocket and his fingers fell on the smaller key he found in Walter Benson's drawer. Pulling it out, he turned it over in his palm.

To say something to break the silence, he said, "I found this at Walter's place, but it didn't fit the file cabinet at his apartment."

"It's probably for his file cabinet upstairs."

Thibault looked puzzled.

"Underneath each desk in the carrel room is a file cabinet. Maybe you didn't see them because they are hidden by the partitions."

"Show me," he said.

They avoided the Werners going back by walking over to another wing, taking the stairs up to the second floor and working their way over to the carrel room. Walter Benson's unit was like the other eleven built four to a row with soundproofing partitions between them, each with a file cabinet under the plastic laminate desktop. Thibault sat down and, using the key, opened the top file drawer. It was almost full of manila folders with names on them. The names he had seen in the appointment book.

"Who *are* these people?" he asked reaching for a folder full of sheets of notations and numbers.

"They're not people. They're animals. These are observation notes on animals. See, Sandy, she's the dominant rhesus female in her group. Red T. is the dominant female for the other rhesus group. Among other things, Walter was doing a paper on female hierarchies in rhesus."

"How do you know so much about his work?"

"It's my job. I interviewed him for the Colter Primate Center newsletter."

"Is it the only work you did together?"

"What does that mean?" She gave him a look.

"Don't get all riled! What I meant is: is that all the work you did together? For someone who shoots from the hip, you can be awful touchy yourself," he said.

"I'm from New Jersey, remember?" she answered shortly.

"Pardon me, but I don't think that's carte blanche for an attitude."

They stared at one another a moment. No apologies were made.

"Anyway, someone from the Women and Gender Studies Department saw the newsletter and got interested in his work, so I helped write up a layperson's version for their publication." She turned back to the folders. "Anyway, this is what his notes looked like."

It explained the entries in his calendar. Times and days to observe animals. Thibault laughed at himself. He had thought the appointment book listed names and dates with women. He flipped through a few files, and they all looked the same to him, with pages of columns of figures with notations in the margins.

He opened the bottom drawer and Gemma let out a gasp. It was also full of folders, but these had more recognizable names on them. Klaus Werner, Beatrice Werner, Victor Allen, Tyler Phillips, Paige Hammond, and about fifteen other names, some of which he recognized from the student interviews and some he did not know. There was even a file on Gemma. "What's this?"

She made a grab for the file and opened it quickly.

Thibault took if from her without much protest, saying, "There's nothing worth reading here except a newspaper clipping announcing your hire at Colter." It wasn't true; there was another sheet underneath it, listing her address, phone number and the comment, 'Sleeping with Werner?'

"How outrageous!" she said, looking over his shoulder. "And untrue. Did he think he was going to peddle his suppositions to **People Magazine** or something?" She looked over his shoulder. "What else is in these files?"

The file on Jason Abramowitz, first alphabetically, contained a cover sheet with address and phone number and some scribbled words. There were about a dozen sheets of lined paper with times, dates and notations similar to the sheets in the file cabinet's top drawer.

"I don't get it." Thibault held up a sheet. "What kind of dirt did he have on this Jason?"

She looked at the papers and turned them over. "Why, these are Jason's data sheets. They look like original observation notes he took for his work."

Thibault watched as she sifted through the file and then reached for another. "Look. The same thing for Leslie Cameron. Pages of her notes." She put the file down and looked at Thibault. "I heard this had been going on all year. But I also heard Walter was one of the first to complain his stuff had been stolen, so everyone assumed it was someone else."

Thibault ran his fingers through his hair.

She held up the two files. "Wow! It was Walter all along."

"How do you know someone didn't plant these in here? Maybe someone else took his notes, too, and decided to blame it on Benson."

"And created a file for himself and put it in to throw suspicion off?" She thought about it for a moment. "How did the person get into the locked file cabinet?"

"Same way I did. He or she found the key in Walter's apartment, planted the files and replaced the key."

Gemma walked toward the window, her hands on her hips. When she turned abruptly, her hair swung into her face. "So, you are saying it this was done by someone here?"

"Why would anyone outside of you all care about stolen notes?" he asked.

"Am I included in the group of 'you all'?"

He paused. "I can't eliminate anyone just yet."

"And what about Bettina Samuels?"

"One of the workers? What about her?" Thibault asked.

"She used to belong to the Animal Freedom group before she 'saw the light'," Gemma added with air quotes, "and then became one of Werner's strongest supporters."

"Great. When was someone going to tell me that?"

"Is that my job, now?" She walked purposefully towards the door.

"Were you just waiting to pull that little tidbit out of your hat?" he said, although she was already down the hall. He glanced at his watch: eleven-thirty already. He looked around the room and found a carton in the far corner with newspapers in it on the way to recycling. He dumped them into the garbage, took the carton to Benson's carrel and loaded the files into it. He relocked the cabinet, put the key in his pocket and straightened up to go, hoisting the carton on his hip.

"What did you find in there?" Victor Allen asked from the doorway. Thibault wondered how long he had been observed.

"Nothing much," he answered. "I'll have to take these with me." He walked toward the door, but Dr. Allen didn't move.

"Pardon me," Thibault said into a fierce-looking pair of brown eyes. Allen moved sideways allowing him just enough room to pass.

Chapter 12

After depositing the carton in his truck. Thibault returned to the second floor and knocked on the Werners' door, which was closed to the hall. Klaus Werner opened it himself, looked at his watch dramatically, indicating Thibault was late for their appointment, and showed him in. Beatrice, seated at one of the matching desks, looked up, then got up immediately and left the room. Werner motioned Thibault to sit down and seated himself behind his desk.

"So, you realize what you've done here?"

Thibault busied himself getting to a new page in his notebook.

"This whole place is topsy-turvy, police barging in to interrogate the staff, rumors running rampant on campus," he continued the stream of complaints, finally winding down in volume and force and merely looking at Thibault with his chin tilted upwards.

When he stopped, Thibault looked up and asked, "Where were you after the party for Dr. Pierce?"

"Where the hell do you think I was?" Werner exploded.

Thibault closed his notebook calmly and stood. "This may seem like an enormous inconvenience to you, your staff and your projects. However, a human being is dead. Killed right here in this building, most likely by someone who has regular access to this building. I intend to continue this investigation to its completion, no matter who it throws suspicion on."

"Whom." Werner said. Then, after a few moments, "I apologize," and he motioned Thibault to sit down again. The calmer mode did not last long, and he answered the original question imperiously. "I went to bed shortly after the caterers left. Sometime after eleven."

"Did you go out again that night or early the next morning?"

"No, of course not. I went right to bed."

"And your wife?"

"She came to bed shortly thereafter. She's been battling some sinus thing and with the Pierce's visit and the party, well, she was exhausted. And no, we did not go anywhere until we came in here the next morning."

"What was the meaning of Walter Benson's accusations at the party?" Thibault hoped his purposeful, calm façade would have a soothing effect on Werner.

"Accusations?" he responded, picking up a pencil from his desktop.

"I was told he accused you of lying."

Werner jumped in before he could go further. "All right, and now I must tell you, Walter Benson was an unstable person who had difficulty with authority figures, and he transferred most of this hostility to me. Without provocation, I might add."

Thibault said nothing, wrote nothing in his notebook. He just looked beyond Werner's head at the framed diplomas on the wall. Degrees from the University of Michigan and University of Chicago. Honorary degrees from Stanford and Oxford.

"He had a problem with a paper I had published some time ago. I won't bore you with the details."

"No, please," Thibault smiled. "I'd love to hear it."

"It gets involved, but basically he questioned the interpretation of some data in an old paper and was somehow unsettled by it all." He looked up from the pencil and leaned forward. His voice became comradely. "If you were at the party, you would have seen what all the guests saw. And it was nothing new. All of us have put up with almost a full year's worth of his insufferable behavior, the worst of it directed at me."

You said that already, Thibault thought. He asked aloud, "Did he have any enemies?"

Werner snorted and threw the pencil down on the desk. "Scores of them. I can't think of a single person who liked Walter Benson. He was the most unlikable person to ever set foot in the door of this institution."

"I get the picture," Thibault interrupted. "Had he taken any documents of yours?"

"What do you mean?"

"Any papers or notes?"

Werner frowned and seized on the thought. "Yes, yes, he did. He did an extraordinary thing, in fact. He had access to my files, and he betrayed that trust to dig up some old and irrelevant notes in an attempt to discredit me. Since that incident, I keep my files locked."

"Did you have anything stolen recently?"

Werner saw what he was getting at. He slammed his fist down on the desk, sending a pen skittering onto the floor. "You found some missing papers at his house! I knew it! I told Beatrice it was Benson, but she thought it was just my animosity towards him. Ha! It certainly fits the picture of a psychotic person, doesn't it?"

"Perhaps it fits the psychological portrait, but it does not explain why he was murdered and who did it," Thibault responded calmly. "Unless you mean it was someone whose notes he may have stolen."

"Well, no," Werner blustered. "What makes you think it had to be someone who works here? Anyone could have made a copy of the keys to this building. All the Colter keys say, 'Do Not Copy' on them but it wouldn't stop someone unscrupulous from getting one made. You would only need to know someone who works in a hardware store or one of those places to make a duplicate."

"Except someone knew how to cut the power so the security cameras were useless. Had Walter spoken to you about his suspicion you were his real father?"

Werner's face contorted. "What?" he shouted. Then his face became red. "What?" he shouted again. "Of all the defamatory accusations that lunatic came up with, that is the nadir. I do not have any children. And I never had any children." He got up from his desk, walked over to the window, and back to the desk again, displaying expensive pants and loafers. "In addition to everything else, he had to engage in character assassination," he said bitterly.

"What makes you think it was a form of character assassination? Perhaps he thought it a compliment to suggest you were his father."

It was clear Werner could not entertain that point of view at all. He shook his head vigorously and glared.

Thibault stood up. "This was just a preliminary conversation. I may have more questions as we delve deeper. If I may feel free…." He left the sentence dangling, shook hands warily and left Werner to his thoughts.

Thibault had hoped to speak with Beatrice, too, but now he had to find her. He took the elevator downstairs and walked along the corridor. This was a section of the building that had a particularly large outdoor enclosure of rhesus monkeys, or so Gemma had said. It was so large you could see only a few animals from the vantage point of the corridor. One monkey came racing by from around a corner and stopped some distance from where Thibault stood and seemed to be looking at him. Thibault moved a bit from side to side, but the monkey did not respond. What was he looking at? He knew the monkey couldn't see inside; the corridors' glass walls were covered with a reflective coating for insulation. Then Thibault laughed. Of course, the monkey was looking at his own reflection. Another animal came bounding around the same corner and the two wrestled briefly before running out of Thibault's line of vision.

He found Beatrice on the first floor in the animal infirmary checking up on the injured galago that had escaped the day before. She turned at his footsteps and said, "Just a minute. I'm checking his wound." She had partially untied the chewed gauze bandage from its foot and then, fully unwrapping it, took off the dressing.

"I can't believe he's letting you do that," Thibault said, remembering how the animal had bared its teeth at everyone.

"He's a gentle animal, really. A male. The female of the species can be nasty. But my special trick is using medication to calm him down, so he won't worry the bandage too much."

"Do you have such medications like that out here?"

"Of course. We're a licensed facility and Dr. Allen is a veterinarian. We have to have someone on staff who can deal with these problems."

She continued to unwrap the other foot while voices rose in the hallway. "What now?" she said wearily, turning to look.

"It's just gone—can't anyone keep track of anything around here?" It was a young woman berating a fellow student.

"Hey, this is my first day out here this week. Lay off, will you?"

The young woman walked past and, seeing Beatrice looking up, came into the infirmary. She was close to tears. "Dr. Werner, we're trying to clean the cages in the south wing and the key to one of the rooms is gone."

Beatrice put her hand on the young woman's arm. "Bettina, calm down, it's all right. You know Henry has keys to all the rooms. He can open it for you."

"I know, but it seems some people can't remember to put them back where they belong," she responded, looking towards the other student in the hall. "The key to Z's cage is gone, too."

"We took it to the police lab for testing," Thibault said. He recognized the name from the list of workers and Gemma's recent comments, but he had not had the opportunity to interview her yet. Now she was on his radar.

"Oh," she responded somewhat deflated. "But the one we need right now is for the far wing."

Thibault thought she sounded near to hysteria. "Can't you use one of the other keys?"

Beatrice was about to answer, but the young woman interrupted. "No, each room has its own key."

Thibault decided to keep out of it while Beatrice tried to calm the young woman down. "Just go upstairs and have Mary locate Henry. She'll know where he is," she explained.

After she had left, Beatrice re-wrapped the animal's foot in gauze tying a knot towards the back.

"Pardon me, but don't you think it was a bit of over-reaction there?" Thibault asked.

"Oh, yes. But that's Bettina."

Thibault was quiet a moment before making eye contact again.

"Yes. She is *that* Bettina. She was, I imagine, passionately involved in the Animal Freedom group beginning in her freshman year and managed to get a tour out here with a fellow student. When she saw we were not performing experiments on live animals or doing anything to harm them, she actually burst into tears. Right there in the main lobby." Beatrice sounded surprised, but Thibault was not after the most recent encounter.

"She 'fessed up,' as they say, and offered to do what she could to make things right. As it turned out, she decided to work out here and she is an excellent mentor for the other students."

Thibault wondered what Beatrice's experience with super- vision had been for her to make such a statement. Bettina seemed overly emotional, barked at one of the workers without cause, and didn't seem to be able to figure out a simple solution to what must be a recurrent situation. Well, maybe they did things differently here in academia.

"I know it seems strange, but the turnaround was dramatic. And it didn't hurt that people on campus heard loud and clear from her we were not doing dastardly things." She wrapped up the other foot and placed the animal tenderly back on its side in its cage. She removed her latex gloves and washed and dried her hands at the large stainless steel sink in the corner of the room. To the right of it was a refrigerator with a conspicuous lock. He didn't want to cast aspersions on the students, but where there were drugs, well, you never knew what people would do.

"Perhaps we could talk out here," Beatrice suggested, preceding him out into the hall. Thibault wondered why everyone in the building wanted to be outside in this weather. He then thought most of these folks had probably been animal lovers as kids and had to be out of doors most of the time. Here they were, stuck all day in a perfectly climate-controlled environment, no wonder everyone needed a hit of the outside from time to time. He felt the same way to a degree, but he would rather save it for cooler weather.

Beatrice sighed and sat down on a wooden park bench. In this light he could see her skin looked sallow and she had dark rings under her eyes. In front of them was a small fountain he had not seen from upstairs because of the heavy tree canopy. The vegetation was so dense he couldn't even make out the opposite wall for all the low shrubs and tall ferns in between.

"Dr. Winkelman had this courtyard landscaped as an afterthought," Beatrice said. "He was trying to approximate a rainforest. I think he succeeded, don't you?"

Thibault agreed, having no first-hand experience of what a rainforest really looked like except from television documentaries, and it had an abundance of vegetation, was hot and humid. Beatrice sat calmly with her hands resting in her lap, the large white collar on her black dress making her look somewhat like a nun. Thibault knew little about fashion but thought the black dress made her look tired and ill.

"What did you do after Dr. Pierce's party?" he began.

"I helped the caterers clean up and then went up to bed. Around eleven."

"Was your husband with you?"

"He had gone up a bit earlier. He was still awake when I went up. By the time I got into bed he was already asleep."

A towhee scratched around in the leaf litter at the base of a nearby tree. With the overcast lighting the bird blended in perfectly, only visible by its movements. The shade and the splashing of the little fountain did little to diminish the reality of heat, however, and Thibault had wished he had insisted on talking inside.

"When did you come in the next morning?"

"I had left home just after seven." She turned to look at him, and he noticed her eyes were so dark there was little distinction between the iris and the pupil. "Klaus and I seldom come in at the same time, and even then, we rarely take one car. We each have many committees on which we serve at the University, and we usually need to go back and forth to the campus during the day. We also teach one class each, at different times and different buildings, of course." She stopped as though wondering if this was too much explaining. "We're energy conscious and I still feel guilty about using two cars," she added.

"Back to that morning," he prompted. He noticed the light perspiration on her forehead and wondered if perhaps she really was ill.

Again, a sigh. "Klaus tried to call me while I was on the road, but I didn't answer. I don't have one of those Bluetooth speaker devices. I thought I'd call him when I parked the car but he didn't pick up, so I continued on my usual routine. I came in and headed for Z's enclosure, hoping to find she had delivered during the night. Instead—," she stopped. She took a handkerchief out of her dress pocket and dabbed her upper lip and forehead. Then she waved it listlessly in front of her face. "I saw Henry Simmons with the outer door of Z's cage open. I raced forward, thinking, 'What is he doing? He'll scare her,' when I saw what it was he was looking at." She paused for a deep breath. "He, Henry, was just standing there, transfixed."

"Where was the body at that time?"

"It was in the cage."

"He told me why he moved the body, but why did you turn him over? Surely you could have checked for life signs in the position he was in, you know it's important not to disturb the body when a suspicious death has taken place?" He didn't know why he said this. It was a bit harsh and pointless after the fact.

"Yes, I know, I know. I turned him over to see if he was still breathing and it was hard to tell with the sawdust up around his face. Henry told me he had already checked, but I didn't know if he was calm enough to have done so. I was afraid the sawdust was interfering with him being able to breathe."

"Okay, then what?"

"I told Henry I would call 911. I didn't know he had already called Klaus, too."

"He called your husband before he called 911?"

"Yes."

Thibault made a note to go back over the notes he had made on Henry Simmons, but their two stories sounded similar at this point. "Why didn't he call 911 right away?"

"It was the protocol we had established in the case of any emergency. We didn't want anyone, mostly young students, to get flustered by something which might be minor and have them call 911. We wanted to control any panic. As you saw."

It was Thibault's turn to sigh. "What can you tell me about Walter Benson?"

"He was Klaus's student, not mine. I never warmed to him much. He came on too strong, too sure of himself."

She seemed to want to say much more, so Thibault said nothing and waited for the silence to build.

"Scientific research is a slow and careful business," she continued, "and he wanted to burst in and 'discover' something. It's not how it's done. You build slowly and deliberately upon the research of all those before you, and little by little a body of work is formed. He may have understood it intellectually, but emotionally he was a bit immature."

The air seemed to get closer around them and Thibault could feel the armpits of his shirt getting wet. He wondered if he still had a spare shirt in his desk drawer in the office.

"Everyone expected Klaus to take Walter's attacks lying down. As if he were too young to know what he was saying, too inexperienced. Walter Benson knew perfectly well what he was doing. He was out to destroy Klaus's reputation by any means whatsoever."

"Why was he so hostile?"

"I don't know. They hit it off wonderfully at first, and then Walter developed this animosity, a grudge, for no reason I could see. You've seen how emotionally fragile some of these young people are. But with Walter I think he had devised a plan before he even got here."

"Plan?"

"To discredit a major name in the field," she said.

"I'm sorry. I'm lost."

She regarded him impatiently. "Instead of doing an original inquiry, Walter decided to discredit existing work to make his name. Of course, when he couldn't find a legitimate way of doing so, he tried alternative means. I tell you, I never trusted him. I always kept my files locked, but Klaus was too trusting for that."

Thibault looked wary. Werner hardly seemed like a trusting person at all.

She saw his reaction and countered it. "He didn't see Walter lurking around the way I did." She pursed her lips as if to stop them from saying more. Her color was splotchy, and she began to fan herself with her handkerchief again.

Thibault remembered Gemma had said something about original research Walter was doing with female rhesus monkeys. Was that what she was talking about? From her description of it getting in the newsletter, it sounded very public and not destructive. "Was this about the female rhesus?"

"No," she answered impatiently.

He looked over his notes again and thought he would talk to her again when she wasn't looking so peaked and most definitely inside the building. He stood, indicating they were done, and she stood also.

"I hope this doesn't offend you," he said. "But it's said

when people are too much alike, they often have trouble getting along."

"If you are suggesting Klaus and Walter were similar, I do resent that comment. And I believe it to be untrue in this case." She brushed off her dress and then fanned herself more vigorously.

"In fact, were you aware Walter Benson believed Klaus Werner to be his father?"

Beatrice was still and stopped fanning herself. As her knees crumpled. she grabbed onto Thibault's arm, nearly pulling him on top of her as she fell to the ground.

Chapter 13

By the time Thibault had extricated himself and helped Beatrice onto a chair in the hallway, Werner was trotting towards them.

"What happened?"

Beatrice had her legs splayed out in front and her head lowered towards her knees. At the sound of Werner's voice, she pulled her pale face upwards and managed a smile.

"What happened?" he repeated as he knelt by her side, looking to Thibault for an answer.

"I haven't had anything to eat today. I suppose the heat was too much," she said weakly. She was making an effort to breathe in slowly and steadily and put her head between her knees again.

A small group had assembled—Gemma, Henry, several student workers and Bettina, who gasped theatrically loudly.

"Get her some water," Werner said over his shoulder and Gemma went quickly towards the kitchen to do so.

"Now, don't get excited. Nothing is the matter. A little sinus infection, lack of food and too much heat."

Thibault looked at the clock on the wall and realized he would be late for his appointment with the Bensons. He glanced down at his watch and saw the hall clock was about eight minutes fast; it gave him the cushion of time he needed. As he wondered how he was going to leave gracefully, Werner dismissed him without rancor, "Thank you. I think you've done enough."

"Shall we call 911?" Bettina asked.

"No," Werner and Beatrice replied simultaneously.

Thibault was more than happy to leave. He bumped down the dirt road, wondering what these chuckholes were doing to his truck's suspension. He slowed down for one particularly large ditch and was glad he had, because a car was coming fast from the other direction. Both drivers braked quickly and the other one backed up into one of the turnouts. Thibault moved slowly by and signaled thanks to Paige at the wheel and a sour-faced Ty beside her. It was exactly what he imagined she would be driving. It was fairly new, sporty and spotlessly clean. He had created an entire backstory for her: country club background, cotillion of some sort, genteel money. His picture of Ty's background was of a surly, entitled teenager who had bullied his parents into supporting him. He had to laugh at this, only because his impressions were entirely formed by his innate mistrust of both of them. But by acknowledging it, he would be more diligent in not acting on his prejudices.

The Bensons were staying at the Wannamaker Hotel. It wasn't a modern hotel, having been built in the 1920s, but it retained the charm and most of the fixtures of that era. The Wannamaker has succumbed to king-sized beds and telephones in the bathrooms and was the choice of the well-heeled when they came to town. It was harder to get a reservation there than at the new multi-million-dollar golf and tennis resort near Research Triangle Park. It was also booked for weddings almost a year in advance; he knew that fact from Lallie.

Thibault dreaded talking to the family of the deceased under any circumstances, and having to do it over lunch would be incredibly awkward. But Dr. Benson had insisted, and the other awkward part would be that they would likely insist on paying for his lunch. It felt inappropriate, but after all, these weren't suspects, just the grieving parents who perhaps felt a need to make some kind of final positive gesture. On the practical side, after the Beatrice experience, Thibault didn't want to ask sensitive questions of anyone again on an empty stomach, theirs or his.

Dr. Benson, a tall, slight man with graying hair, met Thibault at the entrance to the dining room and pulled him aside. "About what I said on the phone, I wouldn't like to be misunderstood." He spoke with a soft, coastal Georgia accent, more pronounced in person than it had been on the telephone. He looked around. "My wife will be down in a few minutes." He gestured to a loveseat beside a large palm, and they sat down. He crossed his slim legs and brushed the crease of his pant legs.

"Walter had had some disturbances lately, and, frankly, I was afraid he might do away with himself. When we got the call from your department, that's what we—well, at least I—thought it was."

"You know now it wasn't suicide, don't you?" Thibault asked.

"Yes, yes. We spoke with the Medical Examiner. But Walter was having emotional difficulties, and—it isn't easy for me to say this," he looked down at his hands, "but he had a tendency to antagonize people."

As Dr. Benson looked up, Thibault thought him the antitheses of all the descriptions of Walter Benson. He wondered what the parent-child relationship must have been like, especially in the teenage years.

Dr. Benson stood up and waved to his wife, who descended the few stairs into the lobby. He turned to Thibault and said, "My wife has a different view of Walter, if you get my drift. I would appreciate it if you were cautious with what you say."

Thibault was introduced to Frieda, a small woman who seemed to be present in the flesh only. They made their way into the dining room, fitted out in colonial antiques with waitresses dressed in long skirts, aprons and mobcaps. The menu was partly Old South luncheon food: pan-fried chicken, Maryland crab cakes and country ham with red-eye gravy, all served with two vegetables and cornbread. But there were concessions to more modern taste buds: steamed salmon and considerable vegetarian options.

Dr. Benson politely allowed Thibault to scan the menu and put it down before he began. "I would like to find out as much as I can about Walter's death. And if there is some way Frieda and I can help, we'd be glad to." Walter's mother was a beautiful woman dressed exactly as one would imagine a wealthy doctor's wife to be: expensively but with taste and no flash. Her blonde hair was probably not natural, but the color and style suited her elegant, if detached, demeanor perfectly. Thibault wondered if she was always this calm or if she had taken some medication prior to lunch.

"I'm afraid I don't have too much information at this point, Dr. Benson—."

"Please. Ed."

Thibault nodded. "But a thorough look at the evidence and the report should lead us to look in certain directions that may yield some conclusions." He wasn't really sure what he just said, but he thought it didn't much matter.

"May I have a copy of the report?" Dr. Benson asked as he picked up his water glass.

"Certainly. I'll have a copy sent here if you like or mailed to your home." The family didn't usually ask for it unless they were planning on suing somebody, but not everyone has a physician for a parent.

Thibault ordered the country ham, a specialty of the Wannamaker. It was true North Carolina ham, pink, lightly smoked and very salty. He could never stand the dark maroon, stringy stuff people in Virginia called ham, much less the rubbery, tasteless stuff from the grocery store. Dr. Benson ordered something called the Lite Fare for himself and his wife and, when the waitress had gone, said to Thibault with a smile, "Haven't you heard about fat and salt in the diet?"

The only response Thibault could think of was something glib and inappropriate like, "You only live once," so instead he smiled at Mrs. Benson, who had not yet spoken, and asked, "Are y'all both from Atlanta?"

Frieda spoke with her voice lifting upward at the end of each sentence like a question. "I'm originally from Mississippi. My husband's family is from Savannah. We met at Emory where we both went to school." She picked up her glass and took a small sip of water.

There was an awkward silence and Thibault wondered how he was ever going to get through this lunch. The beverages hadn't even arrived yet.

"One way you could help me is to tell me about Walter's frame of mind these past few months or weeks. Some people here seem to think he may have had something on his mind."

Dr. Benson cleared his throat. "I'm afraid his attitude change was in reaction to something we told him." He leaned over and reached out his hand on the tablecloth towards his wife, but she had turned to look in the direction of the waitress. He retracted his hand and took an audible breath and exhaled. Before he had a chance to speak, Thibault interrupted him.

"The adoption."

"Yes. It was a private adoption out of state and—."

The waitress delivered the iced tea and told them their food was on the way.

"Where was this?"

"Chicago. University of Chicago. When I was a resident and worked in the ER."

Thibault prepared his iced tea.

"A young woman had a false labor. She confided in me she was not married. The father was no longer in the picture. You can see where this is going."

"What was her name?"

Dr. Benson seemed surprised by the question "McNamara. Why?"

"Do you think she was telling you the truth about herself, the father or the circumstances?"

The Bensons looked at each other. "I believed it was her real name, and later when we arranged for the adoption, she signed the papers with it. It was a notarized document. We did work through an attorney."

"And the name of the father?"

"She never said, and we didn't press," Dr. Benson answered. He and his wife stared at each other for a moment as new thoughts clouded the picture. "We had no further communication after the adoption. She was a student and, if she graduated or where she went after that, we don't know. She didn't seem interested in keeping in touch at the time. She never made any attempt to contact us, and we moved to Atlanta the following year. She certainly knew our names and could have traced me through the medical school."

He then said, "I know it was most unusual we never told Walter he was adopted. It was a purposeful decision. We didn't want him to suffer the taint of being different or of people expecting he would have emotional problems. Obviously, as the years went by, it became more difficult, what with everything else going on."

The waitress delivered their meals, and Thibault began to eat heartily while the Bensons picked at their salads.

"What else was going on?"

Frieda responded, "He wasn't an easy child, very high-strung and subject to tantrums. People in our family are so calm and he was quite different. But he was exceptionally smart and easily frustrated."

Dr. Benson picked up. "He was always a volatile person emotionally, so, you see, we were rightly afraid to tell him about his adoption although he must have suspected. This past year, I thought it was time we told him. We considered if he would be puzzled or curious and even angry, but he seemed to take it in stride. That's what we thought at first. Evidently, it took a while to sink in and then he was furious with us."

"You have to understand. He was a bright, driven young man. He had skipped second grade and graduated from high school a year early. But I don't think he was prepared for the stress of graduate school. This Dr. Werner put quite a lot of pressure on him, well, on all his students, from what Paige Hammond told us. Her parents are close friends of ours."

"Yes, she told me."

"Walter and Dr. Werner were having difficulties, and it was affecting Walter's health. He wasn't eating or sleeping properly and then finally his delayed reaction to our news was greatly out of proportion. He refused to talk to us for a long time."

"But isn't it typical for adoptees to react strongly if they first find out when they are adults? Is it because they doubt their parents' honesty in other matters?" Thibault suggested.

"Those are exactly the sentiments he expressed," Dr. Benson said with a wry smile. "We couldn't seem to convince him it was omission and not a lifetime of deception on our part. We thought the best thing to do was to be available for him when he wished to make contact again. Given time, his attitude would ameliorate. And it was starting to resolve itself."

Thibault could see by the way Frieda looked down suddenly at her plate it hadn't been resolved by the time of Walter's death. "Had he tried to find out who his birth parents were?"

"He asked for her name and we gave it to him, although how far along he got with his search I have no idea," Dr. Benson offered. "As I said, we never learned the name of the biological father."

"Do you know it he did a DNA test?"

"He might have, but he didn't confide in us."

"I would appreciate it if you could call me with any relevant information about the mother you might happen to remember," Thibault said, reaching for two business cards from his inside jacket pocket. "On another note, did Walter happen to mention any people with whom he worked? Fellow students or professors? Either positively or negatively?"

Husband and wife looked at each other and contributed names while Thibault jotted them in his notebook: both of the Werners, Dr. Winkelman, Dr. Nagy from the Botany Department, Paige, Ty, and several other names, some of which sounded familiar and some not. The list of names of people to interview kept growing every day.

There was a long period of silence while they finished eating, and Thibault thought he should have had the foresight to have someone page him about forty-five minutes into this lunch so he could make a decent escape.

"When can we begin to get his things from his apartment?" Frieda asked.

"Darling, don't you remember Paige called yesterday and offered to do it for us?" Dr. Benson said.

"Oh, yes," she drifted off.

Only Paige didn't get to do it, Thibault thought to himself. She could tell them all about it when they asked her. He didn't envy the Bensons the long, sad job of packing up the remnants of a dead child's short life.

They then talked of other things, mostly family and genealogies in little bursts of conversation in which Frieda took scant part. Thibault discovered he had gone to school at University of North Carolina with one of Dr. Benson's cousins-in-law. They talked about the Piedmont area and how it had changed and then how big Atlanta had grown. If the bill had come any later, they would have had to start talking about football.

As Thibault stood to shake hands with them both, Dr. Benson said, "We'll be staying on through Sunday at least."

"I'll let you know if anything comes up," Thibault promised.

"By the way," Dr. Benson added, "we would really like to see the Colter Primate Center where Walter did his research. Do you think it's possible?"

"I really couldn't say. But I could put you in touch with some people who might be able to arrange it." Thibault couldn't think of a worse idea for everyone concerned.

Chapter 14

Thibault sat in his warm, dim office in Leesborough fighting sleep. Part of the problem was the large lunch still digesting in his stomach. The other part was the atypical quiet which prevailed. Usually, Thibault worked with the light on and the door to his office open, as was the custom in this department. But sometimes, when he wanted to work undisturbed for an hour or so, he would close himself in his office with the lights off. He did this very seldom and only when Mutt wasn't around. Mutt liked noise, activity and interruptions; he said he couldn't think if it was too quiet. Mutt himself was a symphony of sounds—teeth sucking and quiet belching after lunch, sighs and exhalations over weekly reports, grunts and mutterings when any physical activity was involved.

But it wasn't just the heavy lunch and quiet that fueled Thibault's sluggishness. It was having to read Benson's appointment book, full of the days and times when he had observed certain animals. He bent and flipped through Benson's corresponding animal files in the carton on the floor beside his desk as he checked each date starting from January. By the time he got to March he recognized all the animal names, but then the animal Suzie Q appeared for the first time. Maybe a birth? A new animal imported from some other research facility or zoo? There was no corresponding file in the carton. He scanned the appointment book and Suzie Q appeared only twice more, the last time two months ago and then for next week. Was it Benson's nickname for an animal Thibault had already cross-referenced? Nothing close. Or did the file on the animal contain something too sensitive and someone else had taken it? He had noticed Z's name never appeared in the appointment book, yet it was her cage Walter was in when he died. Did it mean he had done observations on some animals without having a file? He double-checked and there was no file for Z in the carton. Did someone take the file? Did Benson have another stash of files somewhere? Or were those gone, as was his telephone?

He took a break to stand up and thought he better get himself a soda before he fell asleep. He went to the basement and bought a can out of the machine and said hello to one of the lab techs who passed him in the hall.

"Hey, thanks for the follow-up on Benson," he said. Then he remembered the excitement about the missing keys at Colter. "Can I get the stick with the key thing back from y'all? I'll bring it back when I go out later this afternoon."

The tech let him into the lab, went towards the shelves along one wall, sorted through some big envelopes, pulled one out and looked inside. "Yeah, this is it," he said as he handed it to Thibault.

Thibault walked up the stairs and had finished his drink by the time he got back to his office. He pitched the can into the trash and sat down again to look through Walter's files on humans. He had to look through them all, for even though the researchers, students and staff present at Colter were obviously more suspect, anyone could have come into town, done the deed and left—as long as he or she had a key. He groaned inwardly at the thought of all those additional leads to follow, but at least Benson had thoughtfully provided the addresses and phone numbers in the files.

These files, which were probably intended to contain embarrassing or incriminating information, were, in reality, quite dull. It was mostly speculation about who was sleeping with whom and, after reading through pages of it, Thibault guessed most of it was fiction. Benson seemed to be obsessed by everyone else's sexual activity, real or presumed. He supposed there was no one he could ask who could adequately answer why, surely not Benson's parents, whom he certainly wasn't going to ask. A more pressing question was why Walter Benson had stolen pages of other peoples' notes. From what he had learned so far, it didn't seem as if anyone was working on the same project or in direct competition for information with him. Perhaps more indirect competition was at play, but was the risk of being caught stealing worth the trouble it must have taken to sneak around filching pages of numbers? And how useful was the information, Thibault asked himself, turning over a page and shaking his head.

Most of the files contained pages with notations, but in some cases actual prose, and in Ty's file, an outline for a paper. Was this why they were no longer roommates? In Winkelman's file there was an envelope with a letter inside. In German. Did Benson even read German? Was he just a kleptomaniac?

Werner's file was the biggest by far. There was a photocopy of a journal article marked with NO in the margins in several places and question marks in others. This was clipped to pages of observation notes. Other photocopied articles, perhaps a dozen in all, similarly marked in the margins, were paperclipped to clumps of observation notes. The handwriting dissimilarities suggested several different people had done these, but they all used the same shorthand notation. In fact, this notation seemed to be used by everyone whose notes Benson had taken. Thibault wondered if there was some book of shorthand, a dictionary he could get to help decipher it. He wasn't going to spend a weekend on it, just a couple of hours trying to figure it out. Maybe Gemma could help him locate such a book, he thought, trying to overlook her annoyance with him earlier.

Thinking of Gemma, he flipped back to her file. He remembered the expression on her face when she grabbed for it. What did she think was going to be in there? She had told him candid, if not damaging, information about many people, including Werner, but nothing about herself. Only natural, after all. She was canny, a necessary quality for her job. Necessary for real life, he amended. He realized he was no longer looking down at the files but was staring at the poster hanging on his wall opposite, the boats at anchor, the sun rising over the ocean at Westport. Maybe he would get to go there this month after all, when it was much less crowded than the summer crush.

He shook himself back to reality and checked his watch. It was almost four-thirty, and he wanted to return the key to Colter so its loss would not create another round of excitement before the end of the day. Somehow, he didn't remember fellow students being so excitable back in the day. In fact, he remembered school being a lot more fun. Sure, it was some time ago, but it couldn't have changed that much. He got his master's while he was working, and it was a different ball game. Older students, all of them with day jobs of some kind and focused on getting through to the degree. Even though all of them, including himself, were serious about their studies, no one seem as neurotic or competitive as some of this group at Colter.

By the time he got out to the Center not many cars were in the parking area, and he was worried he might not be able to get into the building. He deliberately went in via the service entrance, which was unlocked, and was able to get all the way to the north wing without anyone seeing or stopping him. He shook his head again at the lack of security. Even if the cameras captured his image, was anyone monitoring the feed? Earlier in the day there were plenty of people around, but it was foolhardy to have such lax security under the assumption people would be around to stop an intruder. Maybe the theory of someone from the outside was not so far-fetched. All someone had to do was get in the building and hide out until dark. He shook his head in frustration.

"Hey, Bruce," he said to the corridor's only inhabitant, who responded in his usual fashion by screeching at him and lunging at the side of the cage. "Well, who knows? Maybe you are the security alarm here." Despite the noise, no one came down the hall, looking to see what had caused Bruce's screaming. Everyone was used to it.

He went into the north wing and hung the stick with the key on the hook next to the door to Z's cage. He looked in the window and didn't see her inside, so he turned to leave. He put his hand on the wing's exit door and stopped. He turned around and took the key stick off the hook and inserted the key in the lock. It didn't fit. He tried upside down. It still didn't fit. He went around to each of the rooms in the wing in turn and tried the key. It didn't fit any of them.

He took the key stick with him as he mounted the stairs to the administration area. Mary was still there, and she turned at his footsteps.

"Oh, Sergeant. I didn't see you come in earlier."

"That's because I just got here. From downstairs. Is Dr. Allen in?"

"Who's that?" he could hear Victor Allen yell from his office.

Thibault motioned to Mary that she didn't need to get up and he would go in himself. "Hey," he said as he stood in Dr. Allen's doorway. "Do you have a minute?"

Victor Allen looked displeased, as usual, and did not get up from his desk. He held his hand out, motioning Thibault to the chair.

"Thanks. I brought this key stick thing back from our lab."

Allen grunted acknowledgment.

"Well, here's the funny thing. This was taken from the hook next to Z's cage and brought in for testing in our lab. There was no blood or usable prints on it, just some dirt and animal hair. I brought it back today because everyone seems to get excited about misplaced keys and such."

Allen ran his fingers through his beard. "Good, thanks." He held out his hand for it.

"Well, no, that's not all. See, this is not the key for Z's room. It doesn't fit the lock."

"People are always misplacing the damned keys. They take the food trolley into the wings, unlock the rooms, put the key on the trolley, put the food in the bin and then close the door to the room. Then they go to the next room and suddenly they've got two keys on the trolley and don't know which is which. I've seen them do it."

"It makes sense—except this key does not fit any of the doors in that wing," Thibault said.

Victor Allen got up and took the key stick from Thibault. He lifted his glasses up and looked carefully at the key. "That's because this is a key from the south wing. See?"

He pointed to the tiny letter 's' stamped on the back of the numbered key.

"Well, I suppose," Thibault said. "But what was it doing hanging up outside Z's cage if it didn't fit any of the locks in that wing?"

"Good question," Allen said, although he didn't sound like he thought it was an interesting one at all. "At least we know where the missing key to the south wing has been. Maybe the mass hysteria Bettina was trying to create will settle down." He gave a short laugh. He stood there looking down at Thibault.

"One more thing. I know this is a weekday and during working hours, but I was able to come in the service entry doors with ease just now and get all the way into the north wing without anyone noticing me."

Victor Allen did not look pleased. "You did? Goddamn it. Mary!" he yelled.

She appeared in the doorway.

"Where the hell is Bettina?"

"She's gone for the day. The day workers are all gone except Henry."

"Goddamn it," he said again.

Thibault stood up, nodded his head and left through the reception area's main door.

∿

MUTT WAS SITTING up in bed with half glasses on, peering down at the newspaper he held. His face was back to its normal color.

"Hey, you old dog," Thibault drawled from the doorway.

"Hey, yourself," Mutt answered cheerfully.

Thibault sat down in the chair next to the bed.

"How's it going?" Mutt asked, still scanning the pages.

"Oh, yeah. Had to eat lunch at the Wannamaker today. Chief's orders." He kept his tone blasé.

"Who paid?"

"Chief did."

"My ass." Mutt looked over his glasses at him.

"Yep. Things have changed mightily since you've been gone, my good man, with Gustafson in charge. But of course, I still need your expert advice." He cast an imaginary fishing line out towards Mutt's bed.

"Where'd you eat lunch yesterday?"

"Huh? Loretta's, why?"

"Mae got me takeout from Buddy's."

Thibault reeled the line in slowly and Mutt rustled his paper and went back to looking at the baseball stats.

"Hey," Thibault resumed. "Let me run some stuff by you. You've seen the news stories on this yet?"

"Yeah, I got some background on it, but go ahead."

Thibault put his imaginary fishing pole aside and stood up. He walked around as he talked, outlining the discovery of the body, and told Mutt whom he had interviewed so far and ran through the names he thought most relevant.

"Did you talk to me about this when you were here yesterday?" Mutt asked.

Thibault laughed. "I knew better than to do that. But anyway, I thought the idea of an outside person breaking into Colter was ridiculous. Until I was able to waltz right in there late this afternoon without anybody noticing. Someone could wait until night, but at night the gates are supposed to be locked." In any case, it would have to be someone who was familiar with Colter to know where it was, how to get in and so forth."

"Sure, it makes sense to me," Mutt said. He had put his paper down and taken his glasses off.

"Could have been a friend, an acquaintance, a girlfriend or boyfriend, however." Thibault had not heard anyone mention anything about Benson's love life, but maybe there was someone. Suzie Q.?

"What about these gates? Do people unlock the gate, come

through and then lock the gate behind them? Or do they leave it open for the next person?" Mutt asked.

"The secretary out there told me that they were left open during the day, but after hours they were locked, and everyone was instructed to lock the gates behind them as they came in or went out after five p.m. Based on my limited experience with those folks, security isn't taken seriously."

Mutt grunted and scraped his hand across the stubble on his chin. "What if an outside person came in with Benson, in his car? Would that work?"

"Might could. Or they—him or her—followed in a separate car. Once the gates were open, said person could get back out easily enough. Even easier if that person had keys to Colter and the gates. I can't imagine someone going out there with Benson and then bushwhacking through the woods afterwards. They've got Benson on camera approaching the building and then he or someone not seen on camera cut the power."

"What else do the techs have?"

"Not much. No significant tire tracks. No tire prints. It's been too dry, and by the time any of the techs got out there, about eight cars had come in."

Thibault walked to the mirror over the second chest of drawers and fiddled with his hair, trying to pat it into place. "You think I should get a haircut?"

Mutt paid no attention and picked up his paper.

"Keys? Cell?" Mutt asked.

"Benson's keys were in his pocket, but it doesn't mean anything. The main exterior door has access with a code, and it locks behind you, so you don't need a key to leave. No cell, although he obviously had one. Saw the bill for service among his things."

"So. Outside person is still a possibility. Any leads?" Mutt turned a page.

"No." The name Suzie Q flitted briefly through his thoughts. "I'm concentrating on the half dozen or so people who worked around him every day and who developed a healthy dislike for the guy."

Looking over his glasses, Mutt asked, "Why, what did he do?"

"Insulted people, stole parts of research papers they were working on."

"Heavens!" Mutt said, holding up a hand in mock surprise. "Isn't it too dreadful!" He resumed reading.

"No, really," Thibault began.

"Now listen," Mutt said. "I know you've been to grad school and maybe you understand the workings of the academic mind, so to speak, but insulting people and taking part of their papers, whatever that means, hardly seems like a motive to kill someone."

"I know it doesn't seem like much to you. Or me," he added. "But these people take it seriously."

Mutt snorted.

Thibault went on. "It's their careers and lives at stake, as they see it. Maybe somebody just snapped or maybe there's more to it."

"You bet there's more to it. There always is." Mutt grimaced. "Help me upright, will you?" Thibault pulled on Mutt's upper arm and, with a lot of heaving and grunts, managed to get him repositioned.

"I don't suppose Murphy has jumped in?" When Thibault didn't answer, Mutt added, "Gee, I am surprised!"

"Does it hurt?" Thibault asked, remembering his mother's long list of folks with piles.

Mutt gave him a withering look. "What's your next question?"

"The interesting thing is this: I looked at this guy Benson's apartment very carefully. Well, it was just the first look over, but anyway, it seems to me as if files were erased from his laptop and maybe even taken from his file drawers. And yet he had an incredible collection of other peoples' files in his cabinet at Colter."

"Why not at his own place?"

"Well, the thought that had crossed my mind is maybe someone else had planted the files taken from other people. But it involves a lot of planning, and it smacks of a lot of premeditation. Maybe Benson didn't ever think anyone was going to be looking in his file cabinet. Maybe he thought he wouldn't get caught. I'm sure he didn't think he was going to die."

"Or that someone was going to kill him," Mutt added. He looked out the window and scraped his hand along his chin again. The beard was coming in white. "You going on vacation soon?"

Thibault growled in response. He thought about the family cottage at Westport and the constant offshore breeze. He thought about the expanse of the ocean and the boat he shared with his brother that had carried them off on so many good times. He thought about Gemma's hair, blowing in the breeze across her cheeks. He thought about the plodding through this investigation for the next week or so. He sighed.

"What color is chestnut exactly?" he asked.

Mutt stared long and hard at him. "Son, get a grip."

After a minute of scanning the paper again, Mutt asked, "Who had access to the apartment?"

"His former roommate still had a key." Then Thibault smirked. "This is great. His girlfriend, not Benson's but the roommate's girlfriend, sauntered in while I was going over the place."

Mutt raised his eyebrows.

"You should have seen her eyes checking out the place, probably to see what her boyfriend had forgotten to take."

"You think they worked together?"

"Dunno," he said. He thought: *Ty and Paige. Klaus and Beatrice?*

"How about Werner and this assistant you mentioned," Mutt asked. "The PR person. Isn't it what they are supposed to do?"

"Oh, come on." Thibault said. "I hardly think she would kill for her boss. She might be interested in furthering her career, but she isn't ruthless." What a curious thing to say, he thought, because he really didn't have a clue.

"I didn't say kill. Werner could have directed her to ask Benson for the files or told her to retrieve them herself. Hell, if you could get into the computer, anyone could." Mutt and Thibault shared a laugh because it was Mutt who had tagged himself as the computer illiterate.

"All I had to do was touch the screen. Then there's the matter of a murder weapon. I don't know if we've got one."

Mutt scowled.

"It appears the key stick thing next to the chimp's cage is gone. I think someone intentionally replaced it with another one to give themselves some time to get rid of the stick that may have been used to hit him on the head and had either fingerprints or DNA on it." He paused. "In any case, things would be a hell of a lot easier if you were back on your feet again. When are you coming back in."

"A few more days. First, I have to do the deed."

Thibault looked puzzled.

"You know," Mutt said, looking towards the bathroom.

"Oh. Ow."

"You said it. We'll see."

"And then?"

Mutt didn't meet his eyes. "I don't know. Mae and I have been talking."

"Oh, man! You don't mean it," Thibault said. "You're too young to retire!"

Thibault continued to stare at Mutt, willing him to look up.

He didn't. Then, not to be the only one to be made uncomfortable, Mutt asked, "So what about Lallie?"

Thibault didn't answer, just waved his hand in a distracted farewell.

Mae had come out from the kitchen, wiping her hands on a towel, as he walked through the living room.

"Just as cranky as ever," he said.

She laughed. "That means he's getting better."

"I'll let myself out and see if I can come back tomorrow." Then he raised his voice to make sure that Mutt could hear him, "Because I have so much work to do."

Mae gave him a playful shove out the door.

He paused outside and wondered why he wasn't more shocked about the thought of life without Mutt. Maybe he would have a delayed reaction, but no, maybe he was getting used to change, liking it in a way even, looking forward to change and what it could bring.

Chapter 15

Thibault worked at his desk most of the next morning. He was enjoying blasting through the paperwork and, although he had an urge to go out to Colter, he would leave it to the afternoon. Gustafson was urging him to expedite the Benson case, so he didn't have the usual stimulation of moving back and forth among the issues he had to cover, something he liked to do. The heavy vacation schedule and Mutt's absence put pressure on those remaining staff to take up the slack.

Aileen's heels clicked down the hallway and, without stopping or saying a word, she placed a paper in Thibault's inbox and another in Mutt's inbox before walking out.

"Good morning to you, too." Thibault muttered to her departing footsteps.

Thibault read the brief memo from Acting Chief Gustafson, reminding everyone overtime needed to be approved, in writing, before it was taken.

"Said that already," Thibault remarked, recalling the staff meeting the previous week where it was clearly stated and reiterated.

Just before noon Murphy popped his head around the doorway. "Hey, T, Mutt still on the mend?"

"Yup," he answered, not looking up from the mileage report he was filling out.

Murphy stood in front of Thibault's desk and knocked on it. "Come on, man. Time for lunch."

"To what do I owe the honor?"

"I didn't say I was paying. Just giving you the pleasure of my august company." Murphy bowed elaborately.

The intercom buzzed. "Dr. Benson on line five," came Aileen's voice.

"Thank you," he responded, motioning with an upheld index finger for Murphy to hold on a moment. He picked up the phone and identified himself while the other detective sat on the edge of the desk and looked at his hands.

"Sergeant, I called our attorney in Atlanta, who called the lawyer who handled the adoption in Chicago and was able to come up with some additional information on it. If it would be of any help." He confirmed the birth mother's name as Susan McNamara, father unknown, birth date, et cetera which Thibault hurriedly wrote down.

"Thank you very much, Dr. Benson." He was glad neither of them had mentioned a tour of Colter before ending the call.

Murphy looked at him expectantly.

Thibault shrugged. "I think this is a dead end. No one would consider it worthwhile to fly to Chicago to try to find this woman for curiosity's sake."

"Yeah, you're right." He stood up. "Forget it. The ribs are great in Chicago and the music is fantastic, but it's either too cold or too hot."

As they sat in Thibault's truck on the way to Loretta's, Murphy unconsciously rubbed his knees and started asking questions about the case. "What about the Animal Freedom folks? They not only made a mess at Colter last year, they also tagged the biology building at UNC, too."

"I hadn't heard that," Thibault said. "The manager at the Sir Walter Raleigh Inn called yesterday to report someone had called them looking for a Dr. Pierce the other day. I wonder if that could be related."

"Wasn't he the professor who was out here visiting?"

"Well, the manager got interested, for some reason, and said he took it upon himself to call a few other hotels, and they all said someone had already telephoned with the same question."

"It could have been the press or some student trying to find out where the lectures would be. Or maybe some lovesick student," Murphy said.

Thibault looked at him incredulously. "I'm guessing you didn't see his picture in the paper?"

"Just because a guy isn't gorgeous, well built, or a famous former jock like me doesn't mean he has no sex appeal. Sometimes it's about the power, right?"

"No, wait a minute. Suppose these Animal Freedom folks were targeting a big name in the field, this Dr. Pierce? After all, many students knew of his impending visit. Maybe they got Walter Benson by mistake?"

"Hmm. Interesting idea. But then we're back to keys and access," Thibault said. "You know, Bettina what's-her-name has had a foot in both camps. I think I'd better talk to her again."

They had to park on the shoulder outside of Loretta's because of the number of cars in the dirt lot out front.

"Hell," grumbled Murphy, looking at his watch. "It's quarter past. No wonder."

The crowd was not in line, however. Most of them were already seated and, being mostly workers from the road project, they were just finishing up.

"Hey," Thibault said and looked over the day's selections. "Catfish looks good."

As they sat eating, Thibault talked about the people who had been interviewed to date and shared no love for the condescension shown to him by some of the Colter folks.

Murphy finished first and unwrapped a toothpick. "What's going on with you and Lallie?"

Thibault put his fork down. "Is that all anybody wants to ask me about?"

"Frankly, yes." Murphy added his big laugh. When Thibault didn't answer and had resumed eating, Murphy asked, "Well?"

"It just wasn't working out."

Murphy rolled his eyes and shook his head. "Four years? And it wasn't working out?"

"Are you trying to convince me to get back with her?"

Murphy held up his hands. "Hey, I'm just curious, that's all. You're my buddy."

Thibault looked out at the little pine trees in the empty field. "Just because everything seems right doesn't mean it is right." He stopped himself, and then plunged ahead. "Just because your friends like her, and your family likes her and she's the right everything doesn't mean...."

"What about the sex?"

Thibault looked uncomfortable. "None of your business. There was just something missing in general. It's hard to explain. But it was important. It is important."

Murphy nodded. "Okay. Say, when are you going on vacation?"

Thibault shot him a look. "With everyone else gone and Mutt out sick, I don't know. And I've got to make some headway on this Colter business."

"Tough luck," Murphy said as he dug at his lower incisors with the toothpick.

"You know, Gustafson said I could tap someone to help," Thibault said.

"You've already got help. What do you need me for?"

"When's your next appointment today?" Thibault asked.

"Aw, man. Come on. How about next week or something? Hell, I almost bought you lunch today," he added pathetically.

"Yeah, right."

"I'm due back at three o'clock. What do you mean to do?" His tone was not particularly gracious.

"This is something you can impress your next date with: the insider's glimpse of a hidden research lab deep in the deadly woods."

"I already saw the place on Monday, remember? And what's so deadly about those woods? You're not talking about those stories?"

"Some are not stories, you know. And I don't think you really saw all of that forest. It would take about a dozen guys to search it right."

"You want me to go to Colter with you right now?" Murphy asked incredulously.

"Here's what I think is going on. I think someone hit Walter Benson with one of those key sticks, you remember, they hang from a hook outside the cages. The one outside the cage where he was killed was taken in for testing and there was nothing on it. That's because it was not the right stick. Someone went down to another wing and grabbed a stick from there and hung it up outside the cage in the north wing. Someone who knows their way around."

"Hmm," Murphy responded. They had turned off and were approaching the bumpy dirt road on the way into Colter. Murphy hung onto the roof handle as they lurched over and around the chuckholes.

"I was worried about what this road was doing to the suspension, but now I'm more worried about what it's doing to my kidneys." Thibault turned into one of the shallow pullouts. He took only a few steps into the forest.

"Watch out for poison ivy," Murphy shouted from the car.

Thibault zipped up his pants and stood there in thought a moment. Murphy got out of the truck and stood where he could see him. Thibault picked up a small branch from the ground behind him and threw it. It hit a sapling and fell a few yards from where he stood. He tried another branch and realized he was unconsciously aiming it towards a pine, so he closed his eyes instead and threw hard. It didn't go far but it got stuck in the lower branches of another pine about twelve feet from the ground.

"What are you doing?" Murphy asked.

"If someone used one of those key sticks to hit Benson on the head, then he, or she, got rid of it. Can't just put it in the trash. Can't burn it, no one's got a fireplace anymore."

"Chuck it in the forest."

"Yup. Miles and miles of it around here. But if someone were really cool-headed about it, they could have waited until they got to the highway and thrown it out anywhere along there. Miles and miles more."

Murphy blew out his cheeks. "Maybe someone driving along the main road saw something."

"Yeah, in the middle of the night?"

Another car was approaching from the outside road and moments later they saw Paige at the wheel, Ty beside her, slowing down. She nodded to him as they carefully went past, but both of them were clearly puzzled by the two detectives stopped at that particular point in the road. Ty turned around to look.

Thibault laughed as he and Murphy got back in the car. "Want to bet someone is going to be out here this afternoon peering into the woods along this stretch of the road to see what we were doing?"

"What if someone didn't have a cool head and stashed the key stick somewhere in the building, expecting to get it later and either clean it off or dispose of it? And what if they haven't had the chance yet?" Murphy asked.

"It's a slim chance, but we can't overlook it." Thibault answered.

"You're going to look in all the animal cages?"

"No, you and I are going to look in all the animal cages."

Chapter 16

Thibault brought Murphy into the Center through the reception area on the second floor and told Mary they were there to do some follow-up work. She listened to him but put most of her energy into not staring at Murphy, still a local celebrity after all these years.

They walked down the stairs. "Doesn't it hurt your pride to know you're mostly a sex object to every woman you meet?" Thibault asked.

"Yeah, T. It hurts *real* bad."

Thibault reminded him what the key stick looked like in the south wing and asked Murphy to go into each wing and look through the windows of the rooms. He also told him to look into the room from the window up above to see if the stick was anywhere in sight.

"They just cleaned the rooms yesterday, so maybe yours is a futile task. But there may be places less obvious than a cage to hide such a thing."

"What are you going to do?" Murphy asked.

"I'm doing the tough, nasty job. I'll check the outside enclosures and I'll meet you back here at two-thirty."

Thibault momentarily wondered if he could work in a casual walk past Gemma's office but realized he didn't have enough time, so he went back outside and looked around the main entrance, a seemingly stupid place to look, unless someone was counting on the obvious place as being the best place. The front area of Colter was mostly lawn grown long, so he strolled over to one of the cages with the ring-tailed animals. Again, some were sitting peacefully on the ground while others seemed to play tag in the branches. As he got closer, he could see the ones running around were smaller and thinner than the others. The youngsters perhaps? '*Lemur catta*' said the laminated sign above the padlock on the cage. It listed the animals' names, numbers, and their dates of birth. He was quite close now and could smell the intensely sharp, musky odor of the animals. One of the larger animals sat on the ground on its haunches, flattened out its ears like a cat and passed its tail through its hands repeatedly. Thibault didn't know much about animal behavior, but it didn't take a genius to see this guy was clearly trying to threaten him.

"Boo!" Thibault said. The animals in the branches stopped dead in their tracks, and even the group on the ground turned their huge, black-rimmed, yellow eyes on him. He stood staring at them for a short while and then moved away. If the animal had been threatening him to get him to go away, it had worked.

Thibault walked around the rectangular north wing. There was no shrubbery or landscaping next to the building in which to hide anything. Looking up he saw there were cameras but no outside lights, which made it unlikely someone would try to hide something in the dark, not knowing how visible it might be in the daylight. He thought he might get a crew out here to search the immediate woods. One of the patrolmen, Crowder, had tracking dogs he used for hunting. Maybe he would ask him to bring them out soon, although Werner and Allen would probably object. He also made a note to search the interior courtyard where he had spoken with Beatrice. Werner could have buried the stick with the key there, for all anyone knew. He stopped himself and wondered when he had stopped thinking 'someone' and had started thinking 'Werner.'

Behind the north wing there was a small makeshift enclosure that used the cinderblock of the building for its fourth side. Here were two large monkeys with long black-and-white fur seated side by side on a high perch. 'Colobus guereza' the sign read. A slight breeze ruffled the white beards framing their black faces, as they seemed to scowl their disapproval of him. Thibault looked into the cage and along the outside of the glass corridor from the north wing all the way to south wing; again, there was no landscaping next to the building and, therefore, he assumed, no hiding places.

Jutting out from the outside wall of the south wing was a chain link fence that extended upwards and was bent over to form a sort of roof around the edges so the animals couldn't escape. Thibault had thought this, too, was an outdoor enclosure, but as there were no animals in sight, he concluded the fence just separated one area from another. There was a door in the fence with no padlock on it; this couldn't possibly be an animal enclosure. Storage, perhaps?

"Hello," Thibault called out, expecting to see one of the staff emerge from around the corner of the wing. "Hello?" he called again loudly. No response. He looked along the edges of the fence only yielding tufts of grass. He followed the fence away from the building toward the forest and craned his neck to see around the wing, but still, he could see no one and nothing on the other side of the fence. At last, he came to the dense forest to his left and could not see to the other side of the wing. He walked all the way back to the door in the chain link fence and reached up to open the latch but saw there was a padlock on it now.

He was locked in.

Or locked out.

"Damn," he said. Murphy knew he was here. No, Murphy only knew he was outside somewhere. It was also only one forty-five, so he had a long wait. Well, in the meantime he could walk the perimeter on the other side of this fencing and see if anything was there. Walking along this side of the fencing, he could see the enclosure was huge, perhaps half an acre. The forest had not been cleared, and ferns, woody shrubs, deciduous trees and pines grew as they would have outside naturally.

As he walked, the vegetation grew thicker and less light permeated the area. He felt the hair on the back of his neck stand up. Someone was watching him; he was certain of it. He stood still and listened. He heard a cardinal in the branches of a tree and, looking up, saw it was a mocking-bird. He remembered how, when playing hide-and-seek in the woods behind his cousins' house in Mebane, he was always able to sense when someone was looking at him from a hiding place. They used to accuse him of cheating, but it was just a sixth sense.

He heard a rustling in the dead leaves and then all was silent again. Thibault turned his head quickly to the left and saw a monkey looking at him over the top of a tall fern. Yet the instant their eyes met, the monkey disappeared and raced away.

"Damn," Thibault thought. "Either one of those animals got out or I got in." He thought both Victor Allen and Klaus Werner would be furious to know he had somehow gotten into an animal's cage. Locked in, no less. Is this what happened to Walter Benson? Someone may not have tried to trap Benson in Z's cage, but someone had definitely locked him in this one.

He took off his jacket and hitched it over his shoulder with one finger. If there were more animals in here, this enclosure would have to have a feeding station in it somewhere. And the feeding station was likely to be closer to the building so the staff could access it easily. Which also meant another entrance and exit.

Thibault set out at a steady pace checking carefully around him, stopping every now and then, on the lookout for monkey scouts. The animal he had seen earlier was most certainly gone, probably because he scared the poor sucker half to death. Thibault was shuffling his feet through the leaf litter on purpose to give any other errant monkey plenty of warning to move out of the way. But all he heard or saw were birds in the branches above.

The dense forest and knee-high ferns gave way to a less dense distribution of trees and then the undergrowth cleared. Ahead, through the more sparsely growing trees to his right, he could see the glint from the reflective covering on the building's windows. He stepped up his pace since his exit was almost in view and came out onto a wide area, almost devoid of vegetation. He could see the long corridor ahead of him and the door leading to the inside. However, one impediment stood in his way. In front of the corridor, evenly spaced, were boxes serving as a feeding station. And climbing all over the boxes, seated in front of and on top of the boxes, were more than a dozen rhesus monkeys.

From this distance, each monkey looked no larger than a small dog, but he knew that was a misleading comparison. He had seen how fast these animals were and how they could jump, they could climb, and he had heard how vicious they could be if provoked. The fact they were eating could serve as a provocation or a distraction. He was counting on the latter.

Although the feeding boxes were evenly spaced along the outside of the corridor, and all were the same size, some seemed more popular than others. The one to his far left, closest to the wing end of the enclosure, had no animals near it at all. Whether because it was in the shade or perhaps not even in use, he couldn't tell, but it was his only possible path to the door of the corridor.

Thibault moved very slowly to his left, figuring in about ten minutes' time he would be positioned along the fence in the shade, giving him some cover. Then, as the feeding groups broke up, he would slowly make his way up to the door and be home free. As it turned out, he could move faster than he had planned since the animals were so engrossed in eating. One pulled a piece of fruit out of a box and inspected it, which gave another animal enough time to snatch it away. A chase resulted with the transgressor's getting away. This scenario was repeated over and over with different monkeys in the short time he watched them. Sometimes an animal would simply reach in and take another piece when the original one had been taken. Some animals waited until another had taken a piece away from the food box before trying a raid, and this seemed to result in escalated reaction. He knew dominance probably played a large part in who could get away with blatant thievery, but he couldn't tell the animals apart, much less which were males and which were females. Some, of course, had infants riding on their backs like little jockeys and he assumed these were mothers. Apart from that, he couldn't distinguish much. Many glanced at him from time to time, but they must have been familiar enough with humans that they didn't pay him much attention.

One back-riding monkey hopped off as soon as his mother sat down. He played around her, pouncing on things in the leaves or yanking her fur. As soon as she began to get up, the little monkey would dash to her and scramble onto her back. A few times the youngster got either bold or too involved in what he was doing to see his mother had moved away and then he squealed and ran to catch up.

By the time Thibault got closer to the corridor, the feeding seemed to be winding down. Animals had wandered away from the boxes, leaving one end of the corridor's exit accessible to him. A large group had moved away towards the forest from which he had come, blocking his original entrance point. He wasn't worried about that; it was padlocked, and no one could hear him shout for help way out there.

He was feeling secure in his ability to get out. He moved quietly but quickly along the fence, noticing some animals had taken an interest in him. They were seated in the grass, picking at it, looking in his direction without apparent curiosity or fear. He decided he was no threat to them, for, after all, they see the humans coming in with food or cleaning their enclosures all the time. Still, their eyes made him uneasy, and several were less than thirty feet away.

He began to move a little more quickly now since his goal was in sight, and a few more pairs of eyes looked up at him. Several animals that had wandered off towards the trees were now slowly moving back in his direction. One, quite a bit larger than the others, moved deliberately to within twenty feet of Thibault and sat down. The animal closed its eyes and yawned widely, showing long, sharp canine teeth. He smacked his lips and turned his eyes to the side.

That sucker is big, Thibault said to himself and then put the thought away as he realized he was becoming unnerved by the proximity of the animals. He hadn't even thought to pick up a branch or stick to protect himself in the event one decided to attack. As he looked around, he didn't see anything he could use.

The seated animal looked back at Thibault, blinked and yawned again. Those teeth could probably rip your arm open, he thought. He reasoned that, if he kept his eyes on this one big guy while he moved slowly, a stalemate could be achieved, and he could make it to the door before any of them got any closer. Thibault was within two yards of the door when he stopped. The little jockey that had been riding his mother's back had somehow lost track of her and had run over to within a yard of Thibault's shoes. The little monkey hopped on something on the ground, turned around and pounced again. Then he froze, looked at Thibault and screamed.

It was hard for Thibault to remember the exact sequence of events afterwards since it all happened so fast. The baby screamed, the mother screamed and came to snatch him to safety while the seated monkey, a large male—as he soon found out—charged with incredible speed. A small band of animals followed suit looking as if they would tear his legs off. Thibault was backed up to the fence with a band of angry animals literally barking at him, ready to attack. He flapped his jacket at them, which drove them back temporarily. He sidled over to the door to the corridor, pulled on it and found to his horror it was locked from the inside.

He flapped his jacket again. "Shoo! Go 'way!" He made himself look larger by holding his arms out and waving them around, feeling ridiculous and panicked at the same time. They scurried backwards chattering at him. Climbing the fence wouldn't do him any good since there was a top to the cage here, entirely enclosing the animals. The monkeys had regained their bravery and were advancing once again. Thibault grabbed a handful of leaves and pebbles from the ground and threw it at them. This time, they screeched loudly. He then moved toward one of the food boxes and saw there were some quartered oranges in it and some kind of brown kibble. He picked up several pieces and threw them towards the back of the oncoming group. The monkeys ducked, but two of them recognized the missiles as food and began a grabbing fight.

"Great. Two out of action. Only twenty-eight more to eliminate," he thought to himself. He continued to pelt the group with oranges, but his ammo supply was quickly depleted. He thought about moving down to the next food box, but there was a chance it was empty and then he would be surrounded with no means of escape.

Thibault ran back to the door and stood with his back to it facing the oncoming monkeys that had begun to bark at him again. He bent to pick up more pebbles and felt a sharp pain in his back. Had one jumped on him?

"Get in here!" Gemma yelled, pushing the door further into his back and at the same time pulling him inside. His jacket caught in the door on the way in, but he released it and pushed the door closed.

"Are you insane?" she said to him. "Those animals might look harmless, but they could have killed you. Or given you a bite with an infection that *would* kill you."

Thibault's heart was thumping, and he nodded his head. "I know. That's why I was trying to get out of there. Someone locked me in from the other entrance and then I got cornered up against the door here."

She looked at him critically. "What? I'm sure it wasn't on purpose. Someone probably had no idea you were in there since people are not *supposed* to be in the cages. Lesson number one, right? It's a good thing it was me who saw you and not Werner or Victor. I still had to go find Henry to get a key to the door here before I could open it."

Thibault looked back at the monkey mob on the other side of the door, now an assortment of seemingly bored animals sitting in clumps on the ground.

"Thanks," he said.

She just shook her head, turned on her heel and left.

Thibault walked down the corridor, glad for once to feel the chill of air conditioning in spite of his shirt being nearly soaked through with sweat. Murphy met him at the intersection of the two halls and gave him a withering look.

"Been jogging?"

"Don't ask. Did you find anything?" Thibault asked him.

Murphy turned to see if anyone was within hearing. "No, but this total nut case girl came at me, yelling about her keys."

"Longish hair pulled back in a scrunchie?"

"Yeah. She nearly tore my head off."

"I believe you met the 'high-strung' Bettina, formerly an Animal Freedom member," Thibault said.

"No shit! What is she doing out here?"

"Interesting question, don't you think?" Thibault wiped his forehead with his forearm and said, "Let's get out of here. I've got to take a serious shower."

Chapter 17

Hours later, as the light was fading, Thibault drove past the rambling homes in the oldest part of Leesborough. He loved the big porches stretching all the way around the front and the vines clinging to the upright supports. The house on the corner of Treyford and McClintock had a huge wisteria, no longer in bloom, but the clematis on the side was, likewise the jasmine towards the back. He thought of Gemma and blamed it on the jasmine scent, although his windows were rolled up and he couldn't possibly have smelled anything.

He continued driving towards Raleigh and a short time later he found himself in the parking lot of her apartment complex, but suddenly his spontaneous impulse felt inappropriate. He waited a moment with the motor running and then put it in park and turned it off. What if she had a guy with her? He got out of the truck. What if she lived with someone? He climbed the stairs. What if she simply wasn't interested? He knocked on the door. What if she wasn't home?

Gemma opened the door before he had time to retreat. "Hi, come on in," she said nonchalantly. She picked up the newspapers strewn on the coffee table and folded them into a wicker trash basket in the corner. "Sit down. Would you like a drink or are you still on duty?" He had on jeans and a polo shirt, as did she, which made the question an odd one.

"No, I'm not on duty. Yes, I'd like a drink. Iced tea would be good."

"Hey, I'm sorry if I snapped at you earlier," she said. "Under a bit of pressure."

"You and me both."

She moved into the kitchen of the apartment, really just a galley area on the way to a bedroom in the back. The room had few pieces of furniture, a small bookcase and a plant.

She brought back an iced tea for him and a glass of white wine for herself and sat on the couch next to him. "What brings you to this neck of the woods?"

"Actually, I was trying to think of some way to thank you for saving my skin. How would dinner at Raphael's seem as repayment?"

"Right now?" She looked down at what she had on.

"You look fine. We'll pretend we're from California."

"Okay. I'm still getting acclimated here, but I discovered it's my favorite place. Just be a second." She took her wine glass with her into the bedroom, and he could see her looking through dresser drawers, taking out a sweater and then brushing her hair. "What happened with Walter's parents?" she called out.

"Oh, you know. Difficult conversation. They seemed real nice, though."

She moved out of view, a door closed, and he guessed she might be changing. He drank his tea. Water ran in a distant sink, and a door opened and closed. She reappeared with her cheeks a little rosier than earlier and a bit more eye makeup and a short khaki skirt.

"How's Werner holding up?" he asked as she took his glass. He was still feeling guilty about Beatrice.

"Quite well, actually. He only bit my head off twice this afternoon." She placed his glass on the kitchen counter and said, "I'm as ready as I'm going to be."

"Haven't you forgotten to put on your jasmine perfume?"

She stared at him. "Is that a question?"

"Some might put it in the category of a request."

Her smile told him more than any response. "If you insist." She went back into the bedroom and came out in a faint cloud of scent. He inhaled and smiled.

Raphael's had been the first Northern Italian restaurant in the area and initially had a slow start when customers didn't see meatballs and spaghetti on the menu. But as culinary sophistication took hold, it gained a following undiminished by the red leatherette banquettes and grape-festooned pergolas from the restaurant's former incarnation as a pizza parlor.

As they got out of his truck, she said, "It would be just my luck to run into Werner tonight. He was angry enough we had lunch the other day."

"First, if I'm not mistaken, he doesn't impress me as someone who goes out to dinner midweek. Second, I thought he wanted you to find out as much as you could from me?"

"That's what I thought, too. But I guess he changed his mind."

"He sounds a bit jealous to me," Thibault suggested lightly.

Gemma shook her head and laughed. "Don't be ridiculous. Klaus and Beatrice are only interested in each other and their work. Not necessarily in that order. But he would be lost without her."

"Third, do you see his car?" Thibault asked.

She scanned the parking lot and shook her head. "We're safe."

Gemma did not look at the menu long before she said, "Sorry, I'm a complete slave to fettuccini, and the seafood fettuccini here is heavenly."

Thibault continued to read.

"They don't have any bacon and grits on the menu here, by the way," she said with a smirk.

Without looking up, he responded, "Now if I was looking for some, I would order the polenta with pancetta or perhaps the spaghetti carbonara. But I'm not in the mood for that."

"Oh, you catch on really fast when you want to, don't you?"

As Thibault continued to read, he said, "You know, you really need to overcome your prejudices."

"My prejudices!"

"Yes, Southerners are all backward and lacking in sophistication. We talk slower because our IQs are lower."

"No, you're right," she said. "Southern universities have produced some right fine basketball and football teams."

He plunged ahead. "They made fun of Carter for being himself and Clinton for trying to fit into the establishment. If he'd stuck to traditional Southern methods in his campaigns, they'd have called him a good ol' boy."

"Who is they?"

"The press. The media."

Gemma rolled her eyes.

"Well, admit it. The press, the media, is based in New York and Washington. Look what the press did to LBJ, picturing him as a yahoo—."

"Now wait a minute," Gemma countered, pointing her index finger at him. "I've read the biographies. He loved to play into the image of a hick."

"And Jimmy Carter. Probably the most well-meaning public servant this country has ever seen. And his entire presidency is dismissed, not just because of the Iran hostages but because he was a Southerner." Thibault realized what had begun as fun was developing into a harangue. "The best they could come up with was calling him a peanut farmer from Plains, Georgia."

"Well, they could have called him a goober farmer, I suppose."

Thibault laughed in spite of himself. "Yankees just think of us as crackers, rednecks, grits, poor white trash."

"So, I'm guessing you've had a rough day, Sergeant Steve?" She smiled as she said it, knowing full well what his day had been like.

Thibault caught the waiter going by and ordered a glass of red wine for himself and one of white wine for Gemma.

"I had a rotten day, too: I am still trying to get the news-letter out and Werner has changed his mind on the text of one long article and the order of the others twice today. His temper is frayed, Beatrice is sick with something or other. The simple piece on Dr. Pierce has gone through six rewrites. I took it home to work on it before you so kindly interrupted me."

"Sorry," he said.

"No, I'm glad you did. I was going in circles with it. I'll probably have to rework it a few more times tonight."

There goes tonight, Thibault thought. He took a piece of warm focaccia from the basket between them and smiled with contentment after the first bite. The waiter brought their wine and took their order.

Gemma continued, "So even though I can write it at home on my computer, I may have to get some stuff Werner said he left on my desk."

"Hasn't he heard about email? You know Victor Allen warned people not to go in after hours."

She shrugged. "I probably won't. It was some magazine piece he dug out of a file that hadn't been digitized. If you work for someone as demanding as Werner, your personal life is over." She smiled all the same.

Thibault changed course. "Let me ask you something that's been puzzling me. If Walter Benson was so interested in Z, then why didn't he have any notes on her? Or files?"

"I didn't know he was so interested in her."

"Well, he was in her cage."

"True. Maybe his stuff was stolen, too. Or maybe he hid it in some secret place?"

"And who the heck is Suzie Q.?"

"An animal? A person? A song? What?" She said it so quickly that, if he hadn't been attuned to her rapid speech pattern, it could have seemed like one long word.

Thibault paused a moment. "Now, first I thought it was a girl, and then an animal after you enlightened me about the other names in his appointment book. But if you don't recognize the name, maybe it was some girl he was dating."

She shrugged. "I never saw him with anyone, but I didn't follow his personal life."

"Let me ask you something else. I keep coming across all these sheets of notations, abbreviations or codes, not just in Benson's work, but other peoples' notes, too. And I can't make heads or tails out of them. And symbols and arrows. What gives?"

Gemma smiled. "Oh, that. That's the famous notational scheme Werner invented, or developed, I should say. It standardizes the observers' note-taking on behaviors. So, one person could presumably pick up someone else's notes and understand the animal interactions going on without having to have the person decode it."

"Sensible idea."

"Before that, every paper on behavior had this long 'methods' section describing how the observation was done, what was being observed and what the descriptive terms meant. Now, under 'methods' people just say the 'Werner notation' was used."

"So, he has a whole language attributed to him. That's cool."

"The beauty of it is, as has been explained to me, you can do a joint project with many observers and the data is uniform and easily analyzed. Werner was also the first one to hit on the idea of using many people for observation, thereby greatly increasing the available data and the reliability of it. Before that, it was more common to have at most two people working together."

"Anyone familiar with this notation can read it?"

"Sure, I guess," she said. The waiter placed a small salad in front of each of them and assured them their entrees would be out soon. When he had left, Gemma said, "Okay, here we are midweek, practically no one in here and it still takes them forever to bring out the food. How long did it take to make this salad, you think?"

"Those little windows in the door to the kitchen are not so waiters don't bump into each other, you know. They are there so they judge how hungry you're getting, and then when they bring the food out, it's more appreciated."

"I never thought of it that way before," she said, not looking entirely as if she believed his explanation.

Thibault continued, "So I was wondering whether Walter had taken peoples' notes to thwart their work or annoy them. Like it's a competition. But maybe he could have been taking them in order to use them for his work."

She paused to consider that. "Such as?"

"I don't know. Was he working on some big project you know of?"

"Aside from the rhesus matriarchy thing?" She shook her head and her hair swung around.

Thibault thought aloud. "If so, he didn't seem to have enough sheets of paper or notes from any one person to do much of anything, do you think?" He stabbed at the lettuce on the plate.

Gemma began to speak in a less rapid fashion. "I know you've been interested in how the animosity between Walter and Werner got started. I've kind of passed over it because there was too much background to explain, but hell, we've got some time now, don't we?" She meant this to sound flip, but when he looked up so quickly, with intensity, she reconsidered.

"Sure," he said, consciously relaxing his tone. "Go on."

She took a sip of wine. "Some years ago, Werner put

together a project on rhesus monkeys. You know, those guys you were hanging out with today."

"Very funny."

"He was at UC Davis at the time and the idea was to observe proximity and degree of interactions of animals and correlate it to the kinship of the animals. To make this project more viable, Werner trained a group of students unfamiliar with the animals in his new technique. This was important, because he didn't want anyone who knew the animals' kin relationships to do the observing and taint the data with their knowledge. He had about twenty students and they did this over the course of a year, so there was a lot of data to work from. Then, and this was for their grade, each student entered his or her data into the program to be analyzed with the kinship information Werner had."

"What was his theory?"

"Simple: related animals hung out with each other more than with unrelated ones." She put a black olive in her mouth.

He thought a moment. "Am I missing something, or isn't that obvious?"

"It might seem obvious, and everyone takes it for granted, but Werner was the first one to demonstrate it was the case. He also had a bunch of associated theories: males were not as closely involved with other animals as females, there was a difference between first-time mothers and mothers who had many offspring, sisters assisted each other with child rearing, and so on. It was evidently a groundbreaking paper that garnered a lot of attention. I say evidently because I am not a zoologist and I have it on his say-so." They both laughed at this.

"But still, he wrote a book based on it, it thrust him into the international spotlight and helped him get much of the funding he has gotten to date. It also put him into the popular magazines and newspapers, you know, "Brilliant, Friendly Professor Shares Fame with His Bright, Smiling Students." In fact, that's how Ty and Paige got hooked up with him. They were two of the group of students."

"Interesting."

"So, fast forward and, mind you, I wasn't here yet, so this is all second-hand information, and Walter is working with Werner's old results with Werner's permission. He decides to go back to the original notes, this time *without* Werner's permission, to see if he can pull some other information out of them. So he says. Instead, he noodles around and can't seem to get the same numbers Werner had. So, he re-enters some of the original data from a couple of the students' observation sheets, which is no mean feat, and sees he is still not getting the same results Werner had." She looked at him expectantly.

"And?"

"Werner got wind of it and cut him off from any further access to his files. But Walter submitted a paper on it to the International Society of Zoology for its annual conference this past winter, it got accepted, and before all Werner's colleagues he said Werner's famous paper wasn't what it seemed to be."

Thibault whistled. "The end to Werner's credibility, then."

"Not at all," she said, leaning back so the waiter could remove the salad plates and place the entrees in front of them. "His theories had been supported by many other peoples' work since the original. What Walter had to say was irrelevant, since he had only gone over a few of the students' work, not all of it, so the effect was merely embarrassing. For both of them. Werner explained it away by stating his goal of using untrained students in order not to prejudice the data unfortunately also produced students who were less than careful about data entry."

To his surprise, Gemma put her fork into Thibault's lasagna Bolognese, and without asking, took off a piece. "Oh, that's good," she said. She twirled a bit of her pasta on a fork, closed her eyes and sighed. "However, this is so much better. Taste it. It's heavenly." He obliged and had to agree.

"Apparently no one dared voice the obvious point that, as senior author on the paper, Werner should have been supervising the students more carefully to prevent entry errors," she resumed.

"How did it sit with Ty and Paige, for example, who were two of those 'untrained' students?" Thibault asked.

"Not well, as you can imagine, but they had been under-grads at the time it all happened. But still, it rankled from what I know of their more recent reactions. Walter's moment in the sun was over when the conference was done and then all hell broke loose. When he got back here in January, when I came, Werner told him to pack his bags, he was out of the program, black-balled for life. I heard all this through the magic of the connecting doors to our offices," she said a bit sheepishly. "Of course, Werner couldn't have him expelled from the University. He doesn't have the authority. But he was able to make Walter's life a living hell. Any friends he might have had deserted him for fear of incurring Werner's wrath."

"Do you think it's why Ty moved out?"

"Ty moved out a lot earlier, as soon as he got wind of what Walter was up to. He was not just pissed at Walter, he was afraid Werner would somehow implicate him."

"If Werner couldn't actually expel anyone, what was the threat?"

Gemma laughed knowingly. "Despite your opinion of Werner as an overbearing man with little tolerance for public officials, his colleagues respect him as the Father of Behavioral Research. If he writes someone a recommendation, they're in. If he writes a negative recommendation, they're history: unemployable."

"But who in their right mind would ask for his recommendation if they knew it was going to be negative?"

"Obviously. But Werner sometimes does not wait for someone to ask him for a reference. He will just go ahead and write one. He believes—and he is probably correct—his opinion, solicited or not, is valuable. He could have done serious damage to Ty's potential career. He would not have gotten his degree, which means no teaching opportunities. No job, no money."

"Along those same lines, if *you* want to be employable in the future, it would be wise for you not to cross the Father of Behavioral Research."

"Exactly," she said holding her fork up for emphasis. "The FBR, I like that."

"At least not in any way he can find out about, I suppose?" he added.

"Correct," she said.

Thibault chewed his lasagna absentmindedly.

"Don't you like it?" she asked brightly.

"Oh, yes, it's wonderful. I was just thinking, though. People who play both ends against the middle often get caught in a tight squeeze."

"I'm sorry. I don't really get sports analogies."

He paused a moment. "If what you say is true about Werner, be careful."

"I don't believe in being careful." She met his look head on. "Life is too short and careful is boring. I did that already."

"I'm not sure we are talking about the same thing," he said.

"Oh, I think we are."

A slow smile crept across her face, and he smiled, too. They ate in silence for a while, yet each time he looked up, she was looking at him and he felt pulled into a wonderful conspiracy.

She pushed her plate away and ran her fingers over his left hand on the tablecloth. "Being emotionally available is an important trait in a person. It doesn't mean there has to be a commitment."

He paused. "Interesting. I think I could agree with that statement."

She looked carefully at him, her eyebrows coming together briefly. "Sergeant Steve, are you like one of your mockingbirds? Ready to sing any tune that is asked of you?"

"Mockingbirds aren't asked to sing a tune; they sing because they want to."

Chapter 18

It was almost one in the morning and still Thibault sat on his porch, the night air warm, but the moon peeking through the clouds from time to time kept him outside. That, and the need to thoroughly indulge his senses which, dormant for so long, cried out to see everything, touch everything, smell everything, experience it all. The farm was beautiful in the moonlight, as if he had never seen it with quite the same eyes. The simple, honest house set in a meadow with trees for shade, and beyond the far fields, the encroaching forest and the darkness.

He inhaled the thick, sweet night air and felt excitement for the future and a willingness to let his emotions go where they hadn't before. He laughed to think Lallie thought he was distant. Of course! She had never made him feel like this. She wanted him to be conventional and steady, he had complied, and it made him dull in his own eyes.

Thibault looked out on what used to be fields of crops many years ago and wondered if it might be interesting to plant something there next year. Corn, tomatoes and peppers would be good, but the rabbits and raccoons would try to devour everything. He could spend the coming winter reading about what to plant and picking out seeds from a catalogue and worry about the critters later. Maybe this place did need a dog. Not just to chase rabbits away from the vegetable garden but to sit beside him on the steps and fetch sticks out of the circle of the porch light on just such a night.

The crickets kept up their cadence, punctuated by the soft noises of a whippoorwill. Far away Thibault could hear a car, an unusual occurrence this far away from the road; then he saw the beam of headlights bouncing off the trees marking the beginning of the wood beyond his empty field. He waited, thinking someone may have made a wrong turn, as people sometimes did. Since his house was not visible from the road or the long drive, they usually turned back almost immediately. No one ever stopped here to ask for directions or for help if they had car trouble. Thibault had the presence of the nearby convenience store out on the main road to thank for that. But these headlights kept coming down the drive. The beams became sharper and bounced as the car hit every small bump and hollow already familiar to him or anyone else who came out here on a regular basis. He sat on the porch and took a sip of his beer, waiting.

It was a small, unfamiliar car which came around the clump of trees sheltering the house from the drive. The driver stopped the car some ways from the house where the porch light did not cast a glow. Thibault stood up and walked down the steps.

Gemma rushed out from the darkness towards him and grabbed his forearms with her cold hands.

"I'm so glad you're here," she gasped.

Thibault led her to the porch and sat her down. "Whatever is the matter?"

"I was out at Center—," she began, but Thibault cut her off.

"What were you doing out there? I thought there were specific instructions that nobody was to go out there at night. Didn't it occur to you it might be dangerous?"

"I know, I know. But I had to get the newsletter done. What I came to tell you is, he was out there." She looked at Thibault with a terrified expression in her eyes.

"What are you talking about? Who?"

"He was out there, I'm sure it was him."

Thibault made her sit down. "Calm down now. Would you like something to drink? A beer? A diet soda?"

She nodded to the beer.

"Would you like to stay out here?"

She nodded again.

As he got up to go inside, she stood and amended, "No, I don't want to stay outside. I'm freezing. He knows where I live."

Thibault turned her shoulders, so she faced him. "Who are you talking about?"

"Klaus Werner. I'm sure he was at Colter tonight, stalking me."

Gemma sat on the wine-colored sofa with Thibault's UNC sweatshirt on, her feet tucked beneath her, cradling a beer in her hand. The light of the lamp beside her threw shadows under her eyes. Thibault sat next to her.

"I'm surprised you remembered how to get out here," he said.

"I almost didn't. I drove up and down the road out there looking for the turnoff and then finally I asked at the convenience store."

"That was lucky," he commented, since some of the clerks were not familiar with who lived where. He was still startled she was here, in his house. He had been imagining it, but not under these conditions. "Are you going to tell me about what happened?"

She hesitated a moment, her eyes tracking back and forth across the huge roses on the carpet as though making up her mind where to begin or what to say.

"Right after you dropped me off, Werner called me to say the newsletter had to go out tomorrow. Why he made no mention of it at work today, and why it has to be tomorrow, I don't know."

"Has he ever done that before? An after-hours work request?"

One corner of her mouth lifted. "Oh, yes." She took a sip of beer and then her monologue picked up speed. "In effect, it meant I had to pick up the document he left in my office, summarize it and enter it into the desktop publishing program right away in order to email it out tomorrow. It still left the printing, folding, stuffing and putting the labels on to those few recipients who require a hard copy. Mary could help with that last bit."

"I was in a bad mood about it," she continued. "Not because I'm not used to tight deadlines, but because I knew it would mean going out to the Center to work on it. I know both you and Victor Allen had warned us against it."

"But I locked the gates behind me on the way in, of course. I parked under the pines so no one could see a car was there or think anyone was in the building. I mean, obviously it was not foolproof protection, but at the time it seemed relatively safe."

Thibault shook his head at her.

She said more defensively this time, "Well, I mean, Walter pissed a lot of people off, but who am I? I only work for Werner. Why would anyone want to hurt me?"

"You forget we don't know who or why anyone wanted to hurt Walter, either."

She took a long gulp of beer. "Well, it's what I had to tell myself in order to go in and get the job done. I rushed up to my office, locked the door to the hall, scanned the Werners' office with the light from my cell, and then locked the connecting door, too. I felt secure and knew even if someone came in, I was locked in and quiet as a mouse."

"The publishing program takes some set-up commands and I had to rewrite the piece and format it to fit. It was going smoothly, and it looked as though I could be out of there in about an hour. Just as I was getting into a rhythm, I heard a click and a whining noise and thought my computer was doing something wacky."

"And then I recognized the sound. I can hear the elevator going up and down from my office. It makes a certain noise when it is activated. I knew instantly someone was in the building and in about twenty or thirty seconds he would be upstairs."

"He?" Thibault interrupted.

"At the time I thought 'he' but I don't know why. Intuition, maybe," she said impatiently. She put the beer on the coffee table in front of them and leaned forward a bit. "I thought about running out to the front entrance before the elevator got upstairs—a long sprint to the car but I had my running shoes on. But then something else occurred to me. The elevator makes noise, so why would anyone take it? Or was I one of the few people who knew that the sound was a giveaway? Then, I thought whoever was in the building had pushed the elevator button as a bluff and in reality was taking the stairs to the upper level. So, I didn't know if he, she, they, were coming up the stairs or up the elevator! Mind you, all this was going through my head in about one-half second's time. And then I thought, the elevator makes the same noise whether it is going up or down, and I hadn't checked when I came in to see if it was on the first or second floor because I took the stairs. Maybe he was right outside my office waiting for me and had been there ever since I came and just pushed the button to flush me out."

Gemma was talking faster and faster and seemed to have trouble catching her breath.

Thibault took her hands in his. "Slow down," he said.

She took a few deep breaths, smiled a bit and they let go of each other's hands at the same moment.

"I turned off the computer, which was the only light in the room, and sat there, indecisive, scared to death, waiting to hear something. But there was nothing to hear except the elevator coming to a halt, the doors opening and then nothing. I waited for a few minutes and didn't hear anything, so I quietly and carefully unlocked the door to the Werners' office and let myself in there. Their office is always locked to the hall at the end of the day, so I felt safe there, but I couldn't be sure whoever it was didn't have keys to all the offices."

"Who does have keys to all the offices?"

"Werner, Victor Allen, Henry Simmons, maybe Mary, I don't know. Maybe someone else? Anyhow, I moved quietly over to Beatrice's desk, crouched down in the knee-hole and pulled the chair in close for cover."

"Why didn't you call 911 from your cell?"

She blinked her eyes and emitted a breathless laugh. "I was afraid I would be overheard."

"Wait a minute—the building has an alarm system," Thibault said.

"Yes, but everyone knows the code. That's how I got into the building in the first place,"

"So, you then assumed it had to be someone familiar with Colter."

"Of course."

"If you thought it was Werner, then hiding in his office was the worst possible place to be."

"Except if it was Werner, he'd look in my office first. Look, you don't always do the most rational thing when you are terrified!" she said.

"No, I guess you don't. Then what?"

"I waited probably no more than ten minutes, although it seemed like hours, but I couldn't hear anyone. As the silence started making me more nervous, I began to think my hiding place was stupid and the first place someone would look, just because it had been the first place I had thought of. And then I thought maybe it was Werner. I thought about moving to the supply closet at the back of their office. And I began to think how long it would take to move there and if there was anything in the way I might trip over or bump into. Just then, I heard the jingling of keys and the door to the hall opened and someone stood in the doorway to the Werners' office because the lone emergency light shone in from the hall. Then he took a few steps into the room and stopped. My heart was pounding. I closed my eyes and listened for something distinctive about the walk and it seemed familiar but for the life of me I couldn't place it. I knew it was a man's walk, that's all."

"Why?"

Gemma was momentarily speechless. "Because…," she began and then stopped. "I don't know, it just was."

"Did you see the feet?"

"No, he didn't come around to that side of Beatrice's desk and he didn't turn the light on, either, thank goodness. It was obvious whoever it was not only had keys to everything but knew to which rooms the keys belonged. I mean, there was no fumbling around as if trying one key and then another, if you know what I mean."

"You mean like someone who didn't know the place well."

"Exactly. Anyway, the footsteps went immediately to the supply closet, opened and closed it. To think I had almost gone in there! Then he went back out to the hall."

"I strained to listen and thought I could hear the footsteps going along the hall on the other side of the Werners' office towards the carrel area, but the air conditioning unit kicked on just then and drowned out any faint sound. At first, I considered staying where I was, but then I thought he might exhaust every obvious hiding place and come back to search more thoroughly. And then I realized I hadn't told anyone I was going out to the Center. Werner was the only one who knew I had to finish this project quickly. And then it hit me: he set up the bogus deadline in an attempt to get me out there."

"Did you tell him you were going to go out there?"

"No," she said slowly.

Thibault thought it over, running his hand through his hair.

"Well, isn't it obvious? The footsteps sounded familiar because they belonged to Werner! I've heard his footsteps in the office next to mine I don't know how many times. That's why there was no fumbling with the keys, he had just unlocked his own office! At that point it occurred to me to come out of my hiding place, go find him and reason with him. But another nagging thought: suppose it wasn't Werner?"

"Couldn't it have been Victor Allen?"

"Victor only comes over to check up on the animals. I've been there before at night, and he doesn't even go into his own office. And he certainly wouldn't take the elevator after exhorting us about its massive use of energy."

"Why would anyone be after you?"

She opened her dark green eyes wide. "I don't know."

"Is there something you know or saw that could point to what happened to Walter?"

Her eyes began to fill with tears. "I don't know. I'm not sure. Maybe I overheard something and didn't think it was important at the time."

He went into the kitchen and came back with a box of tissues he passed to her. She wiped her eyes and blew her nose.

"Anyway, I grabbed Beatrice's heavy ceramic pencil jar, taking scissors, letter opener, pencils and pens figuring, I don't know what, I might be able to use something as a weapon if I needed to, and summoning up every scrap of courage, I went quietly out into the hall. Just the emergency light was on and there was still no sound. I turned right onto corridor and inched my way to the corner, stuck my head out quickly to look down along the next corridor and didn't see anyone. I thought the best thing would be to stand there at the corner because from that perspective I could see from which direction he was coming and at least have one corridor's head start on him."

"Sounds logical."

"I waited a long time, scared to death at first, sweating incredibly, even though it was by no means hot in the building, then getting chilled even though the air conditioning had shut off again. I stood there waiting at the corner, peering down the corridors in either direction, half expecting someone to come rushing out at me from the gloom. But I couldn't hear anything and was beginning to think he had gone. I finally mustered up the courage to walk quietly down the hall until I came to the door of the women's room at the next corner and peeked around the to see if anyone was there. It was quiet and empty until the air conditioning came on again and I nearly jumped out of my shoes."

She paused for a long sip of beer. "Then, out of the silence, Bruce shrieked. I knew someone was still in the building and I knew exactly where he was, too. He was on the first floor in the corridor directly below me. I wondered if he would make a sudden move now his position was given away, and I wondered what direction he would take. Elevator or stairs? I had to get to the second-floor entrance, but it was on the other side of the building, near the stairs. If he was fast, whichever he took, he would be at the entrance before me."

"And then I thought—whoever it is knows the building quite well. He was probably just waiting for me to give myself away, so I decided I wouldn't disappoint him. I kept the scissors and the letter opener in one hand and spread the pencils and pens out on the floor in front of me near the corner. When he hears a sound, he'll come running up the stairs and down this way. Only I was planning on being long gone."

"I went into the women's room, flushed one of the toilets and then ran back out towards the Werners' office, to the corridor and the front entrance. I mean, I really ran. There was a chance he had figured out my trick and was taking the long way around from the stairs. But I can run fast, and

I still had the scissors and the letter opener if I needed a weapon."

"Just after I rounded the corner of the last corridor and with the entrance in sight, I heard a distant clatter and a tremendous thud, which was the sound of a body slipping on the pens and pencils and hitting the ground." Gemma gave a short laugh.

"After that, I didn't hear any more because I was out the door and running to my car, ignition key in hand. I looked back but no one was coming out of the building, but still I wondered if the damned loaner car would start. Thank God, it did. And I raced out of there, stopping only to unlock and re-lock the gate and drove straight here," she finished. She took the last long swallow of beer and looked at Thibault expectantly.

He got up, went to the kitchen and returned with a bowl of pretzels and two more beers.

"Well?" she said.

"Well, what?"

"Aren't you going to say something?"

"Oh." He thought a moment. "You have a really good narrative style. I can tell you write for a living."

"What! Do you think this is a story? Are you implying this is a story I made up?"

He held up both hands. "Hey, I'm not implying anything."

Her eyes bored into him, looking for the meaning beneath the words.

"I only meant you express yourself exceptionally well."

She considered a moment. "Aren't you going to do something?"

He heaved a sigh and looked at his watch. "Well, we could drive into Leesborough and file a report at the police department...."

Gemma got up peevishly and shot him a look.

"What did you have in mind, exactly," he said. "Do you think I ought to go out there and look for someone? Did you see another car parked out there when you left? Do you think anyone is likely to be out there now? And if someone is out there, like Werner, exactly what is he to be accused of? Working late? You were working late, too."

She folded her arms across her chest and looked up toward the corner of the room. He wondered if she was either trying to stop from crying or was trying to make tears come to her eyes.

Thibault continued calmly but kindly. "You can always sign a complaint against him, if you like, though for what I am not really sure."

"Sure. Against my own boss. I don't think I want to join the legion of the unemployed this year." She shook her head and looked down. "Listen, I'm sorry. I've got a bit of a problem. I don't care what you think of my veracity, but I don't feel safe going back to my place tonight, so if I could...."

"Stay here?"

"You have an extra room, don't you? Or I could stay on the couch."

Thibault felt distinctly uncomfortable. "You don't have anywhere else to go?"

Seeing a play of emotions across her face, he backed down. "Hey, it's all right. It was just a question. Really."

He led her upstairs and turned on the light in the simply furnished spare room whose door was down the hall from his. He went to the closet and took out sheets while she noticed a bathrobe hanging from a peg.

"Have a seat," he suggested, as he began to make the bed.

She ignored him and walked to the window, looking out at the moon and the empty field across from the front of the house. "You're really in the middle of nowhere. Isn't it lonely out here?"

"No. I like it just fine. Plenty of family lives nearby. Plenty of company when I want it."

Thibault put on the pillowcase and plumped the pillow into place. "You'd better get some sleep. You look exhausted. Bathroom's right across the hall," he gestured with his hand.

She stood by the window with her arms folded over her chest. "You do believe me, don't you?"

"If you need anything, I'm just down the hall." As he made his way back down the stairs to lock up for the evening, he heard her turn the lock on the bedroom door.

Chapter 19

Thibault opened his eyes; it was already light. He turned to his night table, picked up his phone and saw it was five-thirty. The front door screen slammed and shortly there-after Gemma's car backed out of the driveway beyond the trees, turned around and moved out towards the road. He stood by the window in his boxers and watched the dust settle on the driveway. First, she was too scared to go home and now it seemed she couldn't wait to get away. Well, things always looked safer in the daylight.

He still didn't know whether to believe her or not. After all, who in their right mind would go out to Colter alone at night after what had happened there? Unless she made it up. Or unless she had nothing to fear.

Thibault flopped back onto his bed and reached for his phone again to check his messages, then went down to the kitchen. He saw his UNC sweatshirt folded on one of the stools. He grabbed an orange juice carton from the refrig-erator and took several large gulps, finished the carton and squashed it into the trash. What was Gemma up to? What if Werner had asked her to discredit Benson as much as she could? She had been unflattering about Werner but not accusatory. Well, until last night. What if they had a falling-out or he asked her to do more than she wanted, and she got scared?

He decided to take a long shower, go to Eddie's and have a heavy breakfast to fortify himself for the day. The notion that he could be in an old tee shirt and fishing shorts, getting his arms sunburned on the boat, was becoming more distant.

After a few hours at the department, he decided to drive out to the Center to talk to the two Werners about where they had been last night. As he drove, his mind was turning over issues from the office and he was driving a bit faster than he ought to, but then the driver of the other car had not slowed down either. With a stomp on the brakes from both, his truck and Bettina's little car ended up no more than touching bumpers.

They both exited their vehicles, and Thibault apologized for not reacting more quickly while she burst into tears.

"What? It's okay, it's okay," he said. "You're not hurt, are you?"

She wiped her nose with her hand and slowly calmed down.

"I don't think there is any damage to either vehicle, do you?"

She shook her head.

"Where were you going?"

She stuttered and then blurted, "I was coming to talk to you."

"Shall we go back to the Center?"

"No!" she objected fiercely.

He waited for her to say something else.

"I, I have a confession to make," she began and started crying again.

Oh, Lord, Thibault thought. *We're going to be here all day.*

She sniffed and wiped her eyes and gulped. "I never really cut ties with the Animal Freedom group."

"And?"

"They didn't do anything, and I didn't do anything except pass some information along. About Dr. Pierce coming. It was nothing to do with Walter."

Thibault loosened his tie and leaned against the hot hood of his truck. He looked at a particularly gnarly trunk of a huge loblolly pine a few feet away and let his gaze follow upwards before settling his eyes on Bettina again.

"What did you do exactly? Give them access to the building?"

"God, no! I did it before when the graffiti happened. I did *not* participate in that act of vandalism except to let them through the gates. Anyway, that was then." She chewed the inside of her cheek.

"What information did you give them?"

"I told them when Dr. Pierce was coming," she began.

"It was in the newspaper. So?"

She took a deep breath. "I gave them home addresses for the Werners and some other people." She looked down at the ground.

"Anything else?" He decided to wait her out but continue to look at her face.

"No."

"Well, let's back up our respective vehicles and see if any damage was done."

She stared at him. "That's all?"

"For now." He got in his truck and put it in reverse since she hadn't moved. Getting out, he examined the bumpers and didn't even register a graze. "If you are satisfied your car is okay, I would suggest you return to the Center."

Bettina nodded abruptly, got back into her car, waited until he had moved on before doing a three-point turn and following him at a distance. Thibault blew out a gust of air and drove more mindfully towards the Center, going even more slowly than he had the first time he came out here. Whether it was the strange encounter with the student or his apprehension about having to talk to the Werners again, he really wanted a conclusion to this mess.

As he pulled up to the parking area, he saw Ty and Paige standing out by her car, making him think they could have a little chat. Against all reason, Ty was leaning against the hood smoking a cigarette with all these dry pine needles on the ground. They looked up as he drove in and to his eyes looked conspiratorial as usual.

"Hey," said Thibault in greeting.

Ty nodded his head upward in response. He took a long drag and blew the smoke out of his nose. Paige seemed to force a smile.

Thibault then stood facing them, hands in pockets. "Sure wish this weather would break. We could use the rain."

Ty shrugged. "I kind of like it overcast like this." He swept the lank hair off his forehead.

"Watch out for that cigarette butt," Thibault said.

Ty did not respond.

"You know, it's funny, some people can't wait for rain and other people would do anything but have it," Thibault said.

Ty took another drag and looked the other way. Paige watched Thibault closely but seemed determined not to say anything.

"Sometimes you know someone so well, you think you are going to know their reaction to everything. And then one day, they up and surprise you and say they hate the rain, for instance."

"I didn't say that," Ty answered testily. Thibault could tell Ty had wanted to add something like, *"You stupid cracker."*

"Well, that's true. You didn't say that. It proves my point exactly. People don't often say what they mean," Thibault continued. Ty rolled his eyes. "They assume things about another person and then find out differently later. Like you and Walter, for instance." Ty turned his head slowly and wondered where this was going. Paige's gaze did not waver.

"You're both students in zoology. You date Paige, Walter is Paige's protégé. You both work with Werner. You both need a place to live. You decide to share a place and suddenly he finds out what it's like to live with a smoker. And you find out what it's like to live with him."

"Yeah. He used to get on my case about smoking. I was supposed to smoke on the patio. Not that he ever accommodated me in any way."

"You're right. He seems to have had little success with you. You know, the apartment still smells like smoke although you moved out some time ago." Thibault picked up a stick and began to play with the little ball of sap on the end of it.

"He moved out in December," Paige corrected him.

"Besides," Ty added, "we still worked together. Sort of." He put out the cigarette by mashing the smoldering butt onto the sole of his shoe. "I bet he didn't clean the place once I left. Like I said: he was a slob." He looked to Paige for confirmation.

"Oh, I think you had more of an effect on him than you think. Take his file cabinet, for instance. Each research paper is neatly labeled and filed accordingly. Anyone could go in there and find anything in a hurry."

Ty stared straight ahead, fingering the cigarette butt while Paige's attention was focused on her shoes.

Thibault shifted his weight to one hip. "Now one thing I can't understand is why someone who went to all the trouble of printing out his papers and filing them in a specific order would not also keep a thumb drive of it. Remember," he said, smiling at Paige, "we talked about that. You know, just in case he ever had to use it again or give someone a copy."

Ty shrugged.

"You know what I think?" Thibault continued. "I think someone went into his computer and erased a bunch of files. You can see from the documentation the machine was hardly brand new and it looked like it had had some use but there are practically no files on it."

"But he'd only been here since this year and it stands to reason he'd only want current files in there," Paige said.

"Or maybe he erased the files himself." Ty suggested.

Thibault shook his head, dismissing the suggestion. "Nah. Of course, if it wasn't him who erased the files, then someone has been tampering with evidence." He smiled at Ty. At this point, he didn't see the need to explain there was a big difference if they were erased before or after Walter was killed.

"But I have to tell you that everybody has a backup program. If you erase something, it gets put into a 'trash' file; if you discover later, you erased it in error, you can retrieve it."

"Did he have a backup program?" Paige asked.

Thibault could tell by her question that, if he had, it wasn't available anymore.

Ty's mouth was drawn tightly shut and he pulled another cigarette out of a pack from his shirt pocket. He lit it with a disposable lighter that he put back in his pocket. He was trying to stare Thibault down as he inhaled and exhaled a cloud of smoke to the side.

"As a matter of fact, I was the one who erased the files," Ty stated nonchalantly.

"Ty!" Paige exclaimed in irritation. "You don't have to talk with him, you know."

"So what? They were papers Walter and I had worked on together. We were co-authors. I own them as much as he did."

"What were these papers about that you felt you had to erase them after he was killed? Were you afraid someone would come after you, too?"

"You've got it all wrong," Ty said in an annoyed voice. "I erased them before he was killed. And I'm not afraid someone is coming after me." He blew out more smoke.

"Tell me about it," Thibault prompted.

"Ty," Paige warned, and seeing he was not heeding her, she abruptly walked off towards the building.

Ty noted her exit but continued with some confidence. "Werner was an idol for Walter. He was always talking about him and wondering about him. He seemed enthralled by the fact Paige and I were part of the team who worked on Werner's breakthrough paper. One day we were talking about it, and I was telling him how everyone was trying to guess the kinship of the animals. We weren't supposed to know beforehand so we wouldn't skew the results. Everyone had their pet theory of who was related to whom, you know, just to pass the time. And I said to Walter sometimes you got an impressionistic view of how something will turn out and then the numbers prove you wrong. I said that's exactly what happened to me on the project, and as a result I never make projections about results until the numbers are done."

"He thought it was an intriguing concept: the impression or the innate bias of the observer. He had this idea of interviewing researchers while they were doing a project to get their opinion of how it would turn out and then re-visiting them when the numbers were done. It wasn't a bad idea because a lot of early behavioral observations were subjective in nature. Oh, they were supposed to be objective, but they weren't quantitative at all. And if he could show impressions and actual hard data were different, it would possibly discredit some early research that has been treated like the stone tablets."

"Werner's old data was still around in some old cabinet so he 'interviewed' me on my recollection of how I thought it would turn out. Actually," he added smugly, "I also kept a journal at the time of the project, so I was able to refer to that. Then, because he concluded my numbers might actually have been consistent with my impressions but diluted or changed by all the other team members' data, he tried to trace my data input in Werner's notes."

"Sounds like a tremendous amount of work," Thibault commented.

"Yeah, well, Walter was like that. Anyway, he couldn't trace my data, so he went back to my notes and re-entered the information. His conclusion was I had been right in my original impressions of how the research would turn out, if you were to base it on my data alone."

Thibault didn't follow. "So what?"

"Well, don't you see? It validated my original impression of the outcome of the data. But you're right, so what? It only meant the other team members' data were different enough to cancel out my stuff. Walter decided to interview

Paige, also on the original project, and re-enter her numbers from Werner's files. The more he worked, the more he realized the numbers were not coming out the same as the results Werner had claimed. That's when he hit on his great idea," Ty said sarcastically. "He decided, although Werner's brilliant attempt to avoid the bias of the seasoned researcher by using unsophisticated observers had its good points, it also had its bad points. One very big, bad point. We were also doing the data entry. Walter decided to de-throne Werner by presenting his finding as a paper delivered at the annual meeting."

"What started out as a way to poke at Werner in your mind suddenly turned to stick you," Thibault said.

"Well, no. He was not able to show we were guilty of sloppy data entry since he had not analyzed *all* of the data. And by then Werner had caught on that Walter was digging in his files and stopped granting access. And I didn't want any part of it anymore."

"Because Werner might not approve?"

"Yeah, of course. Werner was on my dissertation committee, and I would have been a fool to piss him off. I didn't think Walter was going to take things that far. I wanted him to remove my name from all collaborative work we had done to date."

Thibault didn't say anything.

"Look, I've worked on this degree for five years, and some kid who wants a moment of glory was not going to screw it up for me." He stubbed the cigarette out on the bottom of his shoe. "Besides, he was not only trying to discredit Werner, who should have been supervising his novices more closely, he was discrediting me and the rest of the research team. I mean, he proved that I hadn't been complicit with Werner, but I could be tarred by the same brush. Big fight. Anyhow, I moved out and we didn't talk for a while."

Ty continued, "Last month, Walter told me he had something new I should see. I had already passed my orals, so I wasn't worried about what Werner would say or do. Besides, I thought Walter was just running his mouth, trying to make up to me. But he had a new theory: the students didn't make the mistakes. Werner had deliberately falsified the numbers to prove his theory. It made sense. I mean, if I didn't make errors and Paige didn't, did it mean all the others did? Of course not. Werner tinkered with the numbers after the fact to bolster his theory. This time I agreed to help Walter, but I still wanted to be discreet."

"Unless it was going to be groundbreaking, too, right?"

Ty ignored the remark. "So, we re-entered numbers from the original research that we could get our hands on, and it was so far off, it could only have been deliberate."

"I thought you said Werner had kept Walter away from the original data?"

"Walter could swipe anything. He had taken all of the original notes months earlier and made copies. He also swiped some samples of other peoples' observations to prove that, while human error was always a factor in scientific research, it was measurable. And Werner's 'human error' factor was off the scale of measure."

"Well, his new theory certainly bolstered your reputation," Thibault observed.

"It's a small academic community out there and you need to be careful. So, you see, it makes no sense that I would want to kill Walter, if that's what you're thinking. If I had done it when he delivered his paper at those meetings, hell, it might have been justifiable. Paige was pissed, too, but she already had a job lined up. Me, I was just finishing up my degree and I couldn't afford negative publicity." He held his hands out as if the logic were evident. "Don't you see? Why would I kill Walter now, just when we're working on the paper that would restore my reputation?" He smiled in conclusion.

Ty's argument made sense. That's what troubled Thibault most of all.

Chapter 20

Thibault left Ty at the second-story entrance of the Center. Did anyone care if Werner 'deliberately falsified data'? Maybe nobody believed Walter and maybe nobody cared enough to follow it up. Maybe that's why the flap at the zoologists' conference seemed to have no long-term effects. On Werner, at least. Only a young, idealistic person would be so consumed about an issue like that. A person like Walter Benson.

When Thibault was writing his master's thesis at the University, his advisor, Dr. Fein, was always available for advice. Once they had a lengthy discussion about Fein's difficulties with his doctoral dissertation in sociology. Fein had studied the family economics on one of the Hopi mesas in Arizona, for which he had to collect figures on what people earned, where it came from and what they spent it on. He knew the Hopi informants used cash in all their transactions and, because there were no receipts as such, they were vague about what went where. There was also another dynamic at work. They wanted to be helpful because it was polite and the appropriate thing to do. But they also did not want to share the information with him because of privacy, possible jealous reactions from others and a host of other reasons.

"Oh, they talked to me, all right," Fein said. "But they didn't really tell me what I needed to know. That's when I discovered what every scientist discovers sooner or later," Fein pronounced. "The Fudge Factor.' If you ain't got it, you make it up." Thibault had shared a laugh with him about it, realizing his thesis wasn't going to need that kind of help. Still, it changed his view of the world completely.

After that, everything he read met with a more critical eye. He saw the census as an enormous guess based on the various Fudge Factors of all the people giving information, or withholding it, and the people collecting it who asked the wrong questions and misheard or misspelled the answers. The National Debt had to be a great example. All the Fudge Factors of all the Under-Secretaries of all the divisions of all the departments of the United States government were combined into one kinda sorta accurate guesstimate. And if the last person to look at it decided it looked too pat, he or she with great panache might add fifty-three cents.

Everybody did it everywhere, it was clear. Thibault did it himself every couple of days when he had forgotten to enter his mileage for the day. Did he go to the Chief and explain he didn't know or remember what the mileage was? Of course not. Fudge Factor. He knew how many miles it was by looking on Google; he just had to make the beginning entry believable. Since everybody did it, why should Werner be immune? Why was it called 'deliberately falsifying the numbers' in his case and 'fudging the numbers' for someone else like Dr. Fein? Not that Dr. Fein had done that, he was sure.

Maybe it was because Werner's face, theory, animals and students had been on the cover of magazines, and as a result of his theory he had received hundreds of thousands of dollars in grants and gotten to sit on important committees. Too much face to lose. While Dr. Fein remained a balding, paunchy sociologist with tenure, little ambition and a good sense of humor.

Thibault knocked on the open door of the Werners' office. The door to Gemma's adjoining office was closed.

"Yes?" Werner inquired, not rising from his desk.

"I was looking for Victor Allen," Thibault said.

"Isn't it obvious he's not in here?" Werner answered.

"Well then, I just have a few more questions for you," Thibault said cheerfully. Beatrice got up to leave but he added, "No, if I talk to you both, it will go faster." He was not invited to sit down but did so anyway. "I have some questions about this paper Walter Benson delivered at that zoology conference."

Werner exhaled loudly through his nose. "I mean, really? Is it the best you can do? Dredge up some old, pointless grudge?" He looked at Beatrice for confirmation of his exasperation.

"You may think it is pointless, sir, but I assure you, Walter Benson did not."

"That's obvious," Werner snorted. He crossed his arms over his chest and with head held high looked down at Thibault.

"I'm sure you've talked to quite a few people by now, Sergeant," Beatrice began, "and they have all given you the same portrait of a disturbed young man."

"No, actually, that's not true. Headstrong, difficult, demanding and immature are some adjectives which immediately come to mind, but disturbed, no. The only thing he was disturbed about was finding out his hero had feet of clay."

Werner continued to glare at Thibault down the length of his nose.

"I don't think he set out to ingratiate himself with you so he could take you down later. I think he started out wanting desperately to be like you and he just wanted to make your paper better. Then he got a bit carried away with the idea of the fame he'd get from debunking his mentor, that's all."

Werner snorted. "How benign and sweet you make it sound. I don't think you understand he was out to ruin my life's work and reputation. I sit on the board of the largest scientific granting agency in this country. People respect me. People ask my advice. No, they *seek* my advice." His voice was getting loud and his face red. "Peoples' careers are made and broken by my recommendation. And this... this *boy* who called himself a scientist fools around with barely legible notes from years ago and claims my students, my own students, were so sloppy as to make mistakes? 'He got carried away.' Do you know he jeopardized the careers of those people, too? For one, Tyler Phillips, a student of mine and Walter's own roommate and friend. Walter had no compunction about besmirching his good name. And Paige, his first mentor and a family friend. To show such undeserved and destructive disloyalty and animosity, yes, it's the work of a disturbed mind."

"You may remember the young are often motivated by the ideas of Right and Wrong, and he saw those errors having been overlooked as Wrong," Thibault said to Werner, who had turned slightly away. "What really bothered him was the suspicion the numbers weren't a mistake, but they had been deliberately falsified."

Werner whipped his head around and both he and Beatrice said simultaneously, "What?"

"That's what he was getting at during the party, wasn't it? Isn't it what he meant when he taunted you by asking what was real and what wasn't?"

Werner's anger dissipated suddenly. He said in a self-assured voice, "I suppose we will never know now, will we?"

Thibault looked to Beatrice, but she was looking down at the hands in her lap. Thibault began on another tack.

"I mentioned to your wife earlier one reason you may have had problems getting along with Walter Benson was the similarities in your personalities."

Werner stood up to his impressive height. "I consider *that* a piece of gratuitous Freudian garbage. My wife never related such a conversation to me because I'm sure she recognized it as such. By the way, I never had problems getting along with Walter. I was his professor, and it was his obligation to get along with *me*. Or 'get along' as they say."

Thibault resumed, "What I was getting at was this: Walter Benson believed you to be his father."

Werner let out a phony, hearty laugh. "You said it before, and I discounted it before." He slapped his desk and indulged in a long, theatrical laugh ending abruptly. "Now, let me tell you why it is so funny. I had a vasectomy—a successful one—which makes siring that viper sometime thereafter quite a feat, don't you think? If you like, I suppose we'll have to call Chicago and see if there is still a record of the operation, eh?" He snorted, shook his head and sat down again. Beatrice did not join in the sarcastic humor. Werner turned and began sorting through some papers on the top of the desk.

Thibault looked up at the wall and saw the University of Chicago degree hanging there. The interview was disintegrating quickly, but Thibault went in one last direction. "Where were you last night from about ten o'clock on?"

Werner did not respond but Beatrice answered for them both. "We went to the symphony about eight o'clock and didn't return until well past midnight."

"Did you go alone?"

"No," she answered perplexed. "We went with the Wassermans."

"What is this about?" Werner asked.

"Your employee, Gemma, said you called her about finishing up a newsletter last night."

"That's right. I called her during the intermission. It had been on my mind the whole time."

"Weren't you aware demanding such a deadline meant she had to come out here by herself at night to work?" Thibault asked.

Werner looked blank. Then he began to sputter an explanation.

Thibault said, "We requested no one be here after dark and you set up a situation where she had to come out here, for what? Risk of losing her job?" Thibault started out trying to make himself sound indignant, but now he was beginning to feel that way. "Had you no concern for her safety?"

"I merely suggested she might want to get it done, that's all. I certainly can't vouch for what someone thinks I said, or how they act upon it," Werner said in a lofty tone.

The adjoining door opened, and Gemma stood glaring at Werner, her hand still on the doorknob. "You really are something. Do you know someone stalked me here last night? Probably the person who killed Walter? And strangely enough, he had keys to all the doors and knew where everything was. And until you came up with the alibi of being at the concert, I thought it was you!"

The magic of the connecting door, thought Thibault.

Gemma moved closer to Werner, the color drained out of her face. She pointed her index finger at him as she spoke. "And it may as well have been you since you put my life in jeopardy. You and this place and all the stuff you put me through are not worth it. I quit!" She turned on her heel and went into her office. She noisily dragged a carton off the top of a shelf and began slamming her possessions into it.

Beatrice looked horrified and gave Werner a begging look.

Werner walked to the doorway and yelled, "Oh, no. You're

not going to quit." He jabbed a large forefinger at her. "You're fired!"

"Klaus!" Beatrice exclaimed.

"Good! Good luck finding someone who understands this publishing program," Gemma responded. "Good luck finding someone who can write two words you don't feel you have to rewrite and edit and write back in again."

"Gemma," Beatrice pleaded.

"GET OUT!" Werner thundered.

"MY PLEASURE!" Gemma shouted back. She picked up her purse and slung it over her shoulder. "I'll be back for my stuff later. In the daylight." She walked out through the hall door.

Werner now glared at Thibault. "Is there anything else you can manage to do?" he asked.

Thibault stood up and smoothed out his pants. "I think that ought to do it for now," he said. He couldn't think of anything else to ask them after that outburst and didn't think he would get any helpful answers anyway. It was about time to check in at the office before the end of the day, but he mostly wanted to catch up with Gemma and apologize for having doubted her story.

Thibault walked outside and saw the sun as a bright globe behind the clouds. There was a prediction for an intense storm sometime later this evening or tomorrow.

He walked quickly to where his truck was parked and saw Gemma's car still there. Her inert body was slumped over the steering wheel of the car. He ran as fast as he could over the slippery pine needles and knew he should check for injuries before going back inside to make an emergency call. But as he put his hand out to the car handle, she looked up. She wasn't hurt, just crying.

He was so taken aback all he could think to say was, "Hey."

She turned her head away and wiped the tears quickly. "I'm not crying because of what I did," she said. "I should have done it long ago and I should have said more to him than I did. I'm crying because after spending two hundred and fifty dollars getting this blasted thing fixed, it won't start!" She hit the steering wheel with the heel of her hand for emphasis and then yelped in pain. She started to cry angry tears and then, catching his eye, started to laugh at herself. "So much for a dramatic exit."

"Here, move over," Thibault instructed. He got in and tried the ignition, jiggled the key, eased it one way and another, but the car made no sound whatsoever. "Dead. Are you sure it's not the battery?"

"Forget it. They just sold me one last week."

"Can I carry you somewhere? Oh, sorry, in your language: can I give you a lift? But to show the depth of my contrition for not having believed you last night, I just might actually carry you."

Gemma laughed in spite of herself, and Thibault smiled at her quick recovery.

"I really do apologize for suspecting you of lying about being stalked," he said.

She regarded him closely. "You never stop being suspicious, do you? What would you be like to live with?"

Try it and see, he said to himself.

As if she heard, she changed the subject. "God, just think how lucky I had the loaner car last night."

Thibault raised his eyebrows. "I think we can safely say it was not Werner. As I said before, it could have been Victor Allen, just checking to see who was there or, well, someone else. I think Werner has a reasonable alibi for last night unless Beatrice and the Wassermans are in on it, too."

"Two elderly professors in the anatomy department are not likely accomplices," she said.

They got in his truck and, with the air conditioning blasting on high, bumped along the ruts out toward the road. "Just because I don't think Werner was out here last night doesn't make me think he's innocent," he said, negotiating around a large hole.

"He's too arrogant to ever admit to any kind of wrongdoing. And Beatrice is his enabler. She's there every step of the way with an alibi or an excuse. She'd do anything to defend him."

After a pause he asked her, "It may have felt good to quit, but it was a bit hasty on your part, don't you think?"

She didn't answer.

"What are you going to do for a job?"

She shrugged and looked out the window.

"Better get your car fixed, job or no," he suggested.

"Here's my solution to the car problem. I drive it back to the dealership—if I ever get it going again—park next to one of *their* cars, lock it up and claim I've been locked out and lost the keys. When they ask which car they are for, I point to a different car!"

"Sorry. License plates. VIN."

"Okay, okay, I've got to iron out a few details. I like the idea of the old switcheroo."

He put on the brakes and looked at her. "You're right, nothing beats the old switcheroo," he said.

"What?"

"Somebody used a key stick to hit Walter Benson on the head. They couldn't put it back on the hook because it probably had blood on it. So, they went down to the south wing, took one of those keys and brought it back and hung it outside of Z's cage. That's why there was all the fuss about keys getting moved and not fitting in the locks."

"I guess I missed that."

"Bettina was twisted in a knot about it. The key stick outside Z's cage that was taken for lab tests had the usual dirt and hair on it because it actually came from the south wing. Then there was no key stick for the south wing cage, that's what Bettina told us."

"So where *is* the key stick from Z's cage?"

Thibault looked out the windshield towards the forest. "I believe Murphy and I searched the entirety of Colter Primate Center. So, my best guess is it is somewhere out there."

Chapter 21

"I just have to check a few reports and stuff and then I'll carry you home, okay?" Thibault said as he pulled into a parking spot in front of the police station.

"Well, I've obviously got nothing else to do today," she replied.

"You can pretend you've been hauled in for questioning for suspicion of operating a stolen car ring."

"Ha, ha," she said, shutting the door.

As they passed the front desk, the day officer said, "There's a woman been waiting on you for some time."

Thibault led Gemma towards his office.

Aileen said nothing as they passed her desk, and she tried hard not to look up.

"My office," he announced, suddenly aware of how small, dingy, and messy it was. The intercom buzzed.

"There's a woman waiting on you in the lounge," said Aileen's voice.

"Thank you," Thibault answered. "Like she couldn't tell me when we just walked past her desk," he shook his head. "Wait here, please," he added, scanning his desk to make sure there was nothing sensitive on it. He opened a drawer and pulled out an old fishing magazine and handed it to her.

"Gee, thanks," she said, taking out her phone and scrolling through it instead.

He walked back down the hall, past Aileen's desk to the visitor's lounge and introduced himself to the only person there. She was rather short, dressed in blue scrubs and thick-soled shoes. A red sweater was over her shoulders held in place by one button. She held out her hand and said, "I'm Suzanne Quinn," and sat back down.

Just then a family of four entered the waiting room, talking in loud voices, and stopped short when they saw Thibault. "Let's go down the hall," he suggested to her, and led her back down the hall towards his office.

Thibault was a bit embarrassed but suggested Gemma wait down the hall in the lounge while he spoke to his guest. The women nodded to each other in passing and then the visitor said, "Aren't you at the Colter Center?"

Taken aback a moment, Gemma answered, "Yes, I am. Was. How did you know?"

"I saw you on television giving an interview." She turned to Thibault. "It's about that I've come." She looked back at Gemma. "She can stay if she wants."

"If it's all right with you," Gemma said, sitting down again.

It wasn't quite, but Thibault made no vocal protest. He gestured the visitor to another chair and said, "Ms. Quinn."

She took off her sweater to reveal a blue nametag from Raleigh General Hospital. S. Quinn, R.N. "Suzie," she corrected.

Suzie Quinn.

Suzie Q.

"You're here about Walter," Thibault said.

"Yes, I am," she said, her brown eyes serious. "How did you know?"

Thibault didn't answer and he heard Gemma emit a little gasp. He hoped it would be the last of her comments.

"He was my son. I'm his birth mother, as they say. His natural mother."

"I suppose no one contacted you about the death, did they?" Thibault scanned her features but saw no resemblance to what he had seen of Walter Benson.

"No. Well, how would they know to? I was supposed to meet with him again, but I was out of town all last week, just got back late yesterday and caught up with the news. I drove over from Raleigh before my shift. I know he didn't tell his parents about me, and I wanted to get first-hand what had happened." She said it in a straightforward manner with no hint of grief. Perhaps her nursing background steeled her for moments like these.

"It appears he died from a blow to the head sometime at the Colter Center. I'm afraid we don't know how it happened yet."

"Was it a fall or an accident?" she asked.

"No. It doesn't appear so." Thibault looked for some reaction on her part, but mostly she seemed to be taking in the information and processing it. "We've questioned a lot of people who had any connection to him and frankly, you're about the only one we couldn't contact. That is, if you are the Suzie Q. to whom he referred."

She smiled slightly. "That's what he called me all right. Strange kid."

"Then I think you have more to tell me than I have to tell you. For instance, how long have you known about one another?"

"Walter first contacted me in late fall. He had been trying to find out information about his real parents for a while with no luck. You see, he knew he was born in Chicago, and he just assumed he was adopted through some agency in the area. What with some of the religion-based agencies not wanting to give out the information, his search turned up nothing. He finally got more information from his parents: that it was a private adoption and my name had been McNamara at the time. It wasn't too hard for him to narrow down the list of possible people from the alumni records. Then he got my married name and found I was here in Raleigh, so close by all along."

She looked around the room a bit. "I have to tell you: I was not particularly interested in any kind of reunion. He called twice before I agreed to see him."

"Why?" Gemma asked. Thibault shot her a look, indicating he would ask the questions, thank you.

"I wasn't embarrassed or anything. But I'm married and I have two kids of my own. I gave him up to a nice couple dying to have a baby of their own. That's how it should be. When I was pregnant with him, I was too broke to have an abortion." She looked at Gemma when she said this. "By the time I figured out my options, it got to be too late. I couldn't have raised a kid by myself then. No way. Still wouldn't. When I signed the papers, I didn't have a moment's regret. I really didn't," she reiterated to Thibault.

"When he called me, I was more than reluctant to see him. Afterwards I thought I should have told him it wasn't me, perhaps he had made a mistake."

"So why did you agree to see him?" Thibault asked.

She shrugged. "I had this whole awkward scene in my head where he shows up for Thanksgiving dinner and my girls are wondering who the heck that guy is. But it turned out he wasn't interested in me at all. He wanted to know all about his father, instead."

"Klaus Werner?"

She laughed. "Klaus? Are you kidding? Walter's father was Frank Newman. We lived together."

"But you knew Klaus Werner?" Gemma asked.

Thibault glared at her again, but she took no notice.

"Sure, he and Frank were friends. And collaborators on a bunch of projects. Klaus. What a gasbag! Well, he couldn't stand me either. Funny how we ended up in practically the same place."

"Why did he dislike you so much?" Thibault asked.

"He was constantly telling Frank, not in front of me, of course, I would hold him back, I was a detriment to his career and so on. I was just trying to get Frank to get out more, to relax. The University of Chicago is a high-stress, competitive place, you know."

"Walter wanted to know all about his father. Were they alike?" Thibault asked, truly curious.

"As I said, I only met Walter a couple of times, so it's hard to say. Frank was a terrific idealist. He would get mad about something and rage about it. He never made it through a day without getting enraged about some injustice. That's why he left."

"I don't understand."

"He got angry about what he perceived as some professor's unethical conduct, and I really can't remember the details anymore, to tell you the truth. He quit school and a month later he was killed in a motorcycle accident. I was already pregnant, and he was gone before my third month rolled around."

They were all silent a moment while she brushed imaginary lint off her lap.

"No one to help you out?" Thibault asked.

"Catholic parents. Nope." She answered.

"What about Werner?"

"The extent of his concern was to make sure I knew Frank had always said he could have his remaining papers and notes. Sensitive guy, huh?" She shook her head. "He probably thought I was too stupid to catch on."

"About what?" asked Thibault.

"Didn't he tell you?" she asked, looking to Gemma. "Walter was going to tell everybody Klaus Werner's most famous theory, his early groundbreaking work was really all the work of Frank Newman."

"You mean Werner took Walter's father's research and published it as his own?" Gemma asked.

"He didn't really steal it as such. He really did give Klaus his permission to have his books and papers. He was done with academia. He may have told him, 'Here, use these ideas if you want. I don't care.' He was so fed up with it all, I'm sure if he had lived, he wouldn't have cared less that Klaus's fame and fortune were because of him."

"So that's what Walter knew about Werner," Gemma said almost to herself.

"I don't know if I've been of any help," Suzie Quinn said, looking at her watch, "but I've got to get to work. If his parents want to talk to me or something, well, I'm here. She took a card out of her purse and handed it to him.

Thibault thanked her and walked her to the front door. "I'm sorry for your loss," he said sincerely.

"Thanks." She gave a resigned shrug. "He wasn't really interested in me, you know. He just wanted to know about his father and Werner." With her hand on the frame, she said, "Poor kid."

Thibault was somewhat dazed by her lack of reaction, but he had witnessed stranger things.

Gemma was still sitting in Mutt's chair when he got back to his office.

"Wow!" she said. "Do you think that's why Walter's phone is missing? Someone didn't want anyone to know about Suzie Quinn?"

"Could be. Or other calls that were made or received."

"And she's got no reason to make it up, as far as I can see," Gemma added. "Just think, she's known all these years and never said anything."

Thibault was not really listening. He was moving towards the door. "Using someone else's theories. Calling them your own. Falsifying statistical data. Basically, Walter called him a liar and a cheat and threatened to make it public with some real proof. I'd say those are pretty convincing motives for a murder, wouldn't you?"

He looked at his watch. "I can take you home now. Or do you want to go back out to the Center with me to pick up your stuff?"

Chapter 22

It was a little past five when they drove up to Colter, but the thunderclouds rolling in had darkened the sky to resemble twilight. The building shone a sickly greenish-white in the unnatural light of the impending storm, and the trees surrounding it had an eerie glow. There were no birds singing in the forest or monkeys yelling in the strange quiet before a storm. As Thibault and Gemma walked to the building, the wind began to pick up, ruffling the lapel of his jacket and flinging her hair across her face. Gemma looked around uneasily.

"Do you think we should go in? I mean, is it safe?" she asked.

He replied by patting his torso where a bulge indicated a holstered gun.

"Oh." Then Gemma took his arm and said, "Look, maybe we shouldn't do this. I mean, maybe I shouldn't be here with you."

He stopped to look at her, but the wind blew the hair across her face, and he couldn't see her expression.

"Don't worry. I am not going to use this." He patted his pocket and she heard a jingle of metal. "But if you want to wait in the truck until I'm done talking to them, that's fine."

She responded quickly, "No, I'll come in with you."

They walked into the service entrance, again unlocked, to the stairs. Gemma looked down the hall at Bruce's cage. "That little psycho probably saved my life last night."

The door to the Werners' room was open and Klaus was there, sitting at his desk with Victor Allen in Beatrice's chair, a cane by his side. Thibault and Gemma exchanged looks. *Had he been the stalker?*

Klaus looked up with exasperation and annoyance. "We're just about to leave," he stated, getting up and shuffling papers on the top of his desk.

"I think you had better make a little time so we can talk," Thibault said, sitting down next to Werner's desk. Klaus sat down reluctantly and crossed his arms over his chest.

"What are you doing here with him?" Werner asked Gemma accusingly as she sidled into the room.

"Vehicular failure," she answered and went to her office and began putting things in her carton, leaving the adjoining door open. Werner snorted. "Don't worry," she said, "I'm not going to make off with any Post-it notes."

"What happened?" Thibault asked Victor, who scowled in return.

"Somebody broke in and in attempting to apprehend him, I was thrust to the ground."

Thibault suppressed a smile. Victor made it sound as if there had been a physical altercation, not a slip and fall. He crossed his legs and said, "I've been giving this problem a lot of thought," he began, looking at Werner.

"Have you now."

"Walter Benson was described to me by many people as sloppy and disorganized, but he did keep marvelous records."

"Oh," said Werner sarcastically. "Perhaps I should show you the notes he took and submitted to me when he was working on the rhesus matriarchy project this year." He chuckled.

"On his personal computer he had several papers in progress that he hoped to use to discredit you. Our own thoughtful Ty saw fit to erase those files. However, he also saw fit to make copies for himself before doing so."

"What was in them, pray tell?"

"I haven't seen them yet, but they are about to be impounded for evidence. You remember we talked about Walter's little file cabinet and all these strange notes I found in them. Especially puzzling to me were all the data sheets he had taken."

"Stolen," Werner interjected.

"Yes, stolen from people. I thought he was just a vindictive little so-and-so out to ruin everyone else's project."

Beatrice came into the room wiping her hands on a paper

towel and Klaus smiled briefly at her. She stood next to her desk and nodded to Thibault.

"Afternoon, ma'am," Thibault said and then continued. "But then it came to me, what he was doing was creating a sample of different peoples' work to see how much error there is in it."

"What?" Werner asked in exasperation, looking over to Beatrice.

"See, I think he felt bad about the paper he wrote about you and the errors he originally said you allowed your students to make. He realized it might have been too simple an explanation. He thought if he were to look at other peoples' work, he might be able to discover something about the error factor."

"My good man," Werner laughed, "it has already been done. It's called sampling error. Every statistical study lists the probability of error. It's a mathematical formula, for God's sake."

Beatrice added, "Yes, even the most uninitiated person is familiar with the concept."

"Yes, I know," Thibault said. "But he was trying to uncover an error factor, not a sampling error. His theory was not that there was sampling error, but the researcher goofed entering the numbers. He wanted to figure out if there was some regularity to this type of error."

Werner snorted again and Gemma stopped her packing of the carton to listen more intently.

Thibault continued, "He felt he was on to something. All along he was trying to find some excuse for the errors he had uncovered in your first team project. All along he wanted to believe it was the students' mistake; he wanted most desperately to believe in you. When he found out it was you who falsified the data, he became a changed person."

"What are you talking about?" Werner boomed. "Since when do you have knowledge of what Walter Benson thought and what he wanted to believe in? You never even met him! And how dare you suggest I falsified the data?"

"You're right about one thing. I didn't know Walter Benson or what he thought. I merely saw his crushed skull and bloodied body on a floor downstairs. But I think you can imagine what he did think and wanted to believe in. He heard all about you from Paige and he probably built up this image of you and what you had done. Just think—the excitement of scientific discovery!"

Werner shook his head in exasperation.

"Yes, an idealistic and immature view of what actually happens," Thibault continued, "but he was an idealistic and immature young man. He came here hoping to work with you, hoping to discover something important. And instead, he stumbled upon the very thing to destroy his ideals. He discovered you had changed the numbers the students had given you. It was really perfect in many ways: none of them knew what numbers the others had entered so when the results didn't work out according to plan, you just nudged the data this way and that."

"That's not true. Walter had already demonstrated it was the students' error." Beatrice's dark eyes narrowed.

"You have no proof," Werner said to Thibault.

"Yes, he does," Ty said from the hall doorway. He took a few confident steps inside and leaned casually against the bookcase.

"Do join us," Thibault said.

Ty looked back into the hall and Paige quietly stepped into the room and stood next to him.

"Well," Thibault said slowly, "he's right, actually. I do have proof." He looked for a reaction from the Werners and was not disappointed. "Walter had based his inflammatory paper about you on information supplied by Paige and Ty and supported by your notes. When he hit upon this new theory, that you had falsified the numbers, he went back to your notes and laboriously reentered the numbers from the students' note sheets. You see, there was no mistake about it. He was pushed even further in his zeal to discredit you when he found out your theory of kinship interactions was developed by Frank Newman, not you."

"Whoa!" Ty exclaimed, and then he added, "Who the heck is Frank Newman?"

Thibault ignored the outburst and continued, "He may have given you his theory and his work before he left Chicago, but you never acknowledged they were not your own."

"What?" Werner said. He looked to Beatrice. She gave him a slow smile.

"Jesus!" Ty exclaimed. "So—who is Frank Newman?"

"How did you find out?" Werner asked Beatrice.

"How could I not know?" she responded.

It was Thibault who explained. "Walter found his birth mother and the identity of his birth father, Frank Newman. Walter was their son."

It took a few moments for the information to sink in.

Paige asked, "So what does that mean?"

"I don't get it," Ty added, mostly to her.

Werner uncrossed his arms and looked at his hands spread on the desk in front of him. "I will admit it wasn't my theory originally, but Frank did give it to me and all his papers. He said I was welcome to them, and he had had enough of the graduate school program. About the other thing...I had been working a long time with little recognition. I knew the theory was right. I just knew it."

Thibault heard Ty's derisive laugh.

"The idea of using untrained students was a brilliant idea, if I do say so myself, and bound to garner a lot of attention, but in fact they did a less-than-stellar job with the observations." Werner looked directly at Ty and said pointedly, "If I had used trained students instead, I am convinced the results would have been borne out."

"Oh, right!" Ty remarked.

"It's irrelevant, isn't it? Since then, the theory has been proved over and over again by other researchers, so you see, I was correct in my original assumption." Werner stood up and looked at the diplomas hanging on the wall behind his desk. He turned abruptly. "All right. I was wrong in what I did. And I have admitted it. So what?" He held his head up.

"Is your ego boundless?" Gemma asked stepping into the room. "Do you think he's come here to talk about Dr. Klaus Werner and his work? He's come to accuse you of murder."

Thibault gave her a look he hoped would silence any further outbursts.

Werner looked as if he had been punched in the stomach and sat down again. He looked to Thibault and then to Beatrice, who put a hand up to her mouth.

"Doctor Allen?" It was Bettina at the door to the Werners' office. "Oh," she said when she saw the assembled group.

"Come in, come in. I think you have something to add to this interesting discussion," Thibault said.

She looked at him, half angry and half scared, but came in, nonetheless.

Thibault stood up and said, "Well, since someone has brought up the M word, let's talk about it. I don't think this murder happened entirely spontaneously, since the power was shut off so there wouldn't be a record of who came in after him. Maybe it was Walter who shut off the power so his movements couldn't be tracked. Or maybe it was someone else. And how Walter and his aggressor both happened to be in Z's cage, I don't know. But my guess is there were the usual accusations thrown around, with the result being that Benson said he could work solo just fine, and suddenly there was no more hold over him. The frustration that had been building for so long was unleashed. Threats were useless and the tables had been turned. But there was the key stick still in the door. It all happens so quickly, and Walter is lying on the floor with a huge puddle of blood oozing from his head. Quick. Wash off the stick.

But perhaps there are some traces of blood or tissue on it. You have to get rid of it. But a better idea occurs to you. Go get another key stick and put it next to Z's cage and take the bloodied one away with you."

"That's a total fabrication," Werner said.

"On the morning of the murder we took the key stick from outside Z's cage and the lab tested it and found nothing. It was only later when Bettina pointed out the key stick for one of the cages in the galago area was missing that I found the key stick outside Z's cage didn't fit the door. It wasn't the murder weapon: that key stick was long gone."

Werner said, "Why are you accusing me? What about these two?" he pointed at Paige and Ty. "Walter tried to smear their reputations, too. What about Victor Allen? Maybe he was angry for some reason we don't even know of. What about Bettina? What about Gemma? What about anybody around here who had their data stolen? Anyone could have had a grievance with him. You have no proof. Furthermore, if you try to arrest me on this charge without a shred of proof, my lawyer—."

"Stop," Beatrice said, standing up. She was about to say something.

"Beatrice, stop protecting him," Gemma shouted.

"Beatrice, stop it," Werner said calmly. "It wasn't I who did it." He went over and embraced her, and she began to cry quietly.

Ty applauded, three slow claps.

"Oh, shut up," Paige said to him.

"Dr. Werner is right," Thibault said. "He didn't do it. Why would he whack Walter on the head when he had more effective weapons in his arsenal? With a few phone calls and letters, he could blackball Walter from an academic career forever. He could make or break anyone. Walter had already tried to poke a big hole in Werner's reputation, and nothing happened. A bit of a bruise, that's all. Werner could probably survive an even greater assault. No, we're looking for someone much more vulnerable than that."

Thibault turned to Gemma. Her eyes widened.

"Someone who had no effective means of fighting back. Now Gemma's got both of the Werners standing firmly behind her, or did, although she sometimes thought they weren't. Taskmasters, yes. But also, supportive, wouldn't you say?"

Gemma nodded her head as if a string pulled it.

"No, you, too, are in a powerful position," he said.

He looked at Bettina. "Your past participation with the Animal Freedom group puts you in the spotlight, however."

"No!" she protested.

"However, I can't imagine that someone as emotionally fragile as you could have killed someone and not felt immense remorse."

She started to cry, whether because of the true things he had said or in relief.

He turned to Ty and Paige.

"Paige's got her job, but she's always been cautious. She wouldn't risk everything for one moment of glory. No,

Paige sees the big picture, all right. And my guess is she tried to dissuade Ty from getting involved in Walter's schemes. And once he did become involved again, she distanced herself as much as she could from the two of them."

"Not that Ty wasn't concerned about Werner's opinion of him and always being able to get a recommendation from him in the future." Thibault now turned to Ty. "You were torn between the tremendous notoriety you would get by exposing Werner and the old fear he might retaliate. After all, you still don't have a job."

"Well, sure, "Ty replied. "It had crossed my mind I could be cutting my own throat. But to be the one who discredits a major theory is an incredible coup." He laughed. "Here I am, following Paige out to California because she has a position, not me. I was feeling kind of depressed after coming down from the high of having finally finished my degree."

"You were planning to use the files to publish this theory with just your name on it?" Thibault suggested.

"No. No, you've got it all wrong. I took the files for protection in case Werner got to Walter's computer first."

"First? You mean you knew he was dead already?"

"No! I mean the night of the party. I got scared he might shoot his mouth off. He'd been threatening to do it all along, and what Werner might do as a result. I also started to think about the extent of Werner's influence and got cold feet. And sure enough, Benson shows up at the party, uninvited, and practically blurts the whole thing out. I thought about calling him earlier to convince him we shouldn't go through with it; it would hurt too many people. Like me, for instance. And Paige." His eyes darted around the room. "Hey, if you restore the files, I bet you'll be able to see when they were removed," he said brightly.

No one said anything.

Ty plunged on. "Walter didn't answer my texts. So, I went over to his apartment to convince him, but he wasn't there, and I took the opportunity to erase the files from the hard disk and take the files with me. Anyhow, I still have all those files, and I really didn't steal them. They were half mine, too. And I was always a welcome guest in his apartment, so I didn't break in or anything."

"You had no other motive for taking the files—such as blackmailing Werner into getting you into a good position?" Thibault asked.

Ty managed a weak laugh. "I grant you the relationship between doctoral candidate and major professor is ambivalent at best, but blackmail? No."

Thibault stopped him. "No, I think you were still scared. Walter wasn't at his place so you guessed he would be out here after he left the party. You didn't know what he was going to do, and you needed to come out here to convince him not to publish. Maybe you thought it was a paper that deserved only one author: you. It would be killing two birds with one stone, wouldn't it? Pardon the analogy. Competition out of the way and major suspicion thrown on Klaus Werner."

"Of course not," Ty responded desperately. "Paige already told you I was with her all night."

"I know. And you have confirmed she was with you. How convenient."

There was a pause as all eyes were on Paige.

"That's not what I said," she enunciated deliberately. "I said 'he was there all night, as far as I know'."

"Jesus—," Ty began. He looked around the room. He flung the limp hair off his forehead. "You don't have any proof!"

"Ah, but we do," Thibault said evenly. "We have the murder weapon. The tracking dogs we employed found it yesterday. They're doing an analysis of the key stick for tissue, fiber and fingerprints even as we speak. What you did with Walter's phone, we don't know since it lost all connection about the time he died."

"Give me the keys," Ty said frantically to Paige.

She looked around the room, pulled the keys slowly from her purse and looked at Ty.

"The keys!" He stuck his hand out, his long fingers splayed in desperation.

The keys flew in a slow arc from Paige's hand to the intended destination. Thibault's outstretched arm.

Ty put his arm across his face. "Christ," he muttered and started to cry.

Thibault read him his rights as the others looked on silently.

"You couldn't reason with him. Once he got going on something, he couldn't stop!" He wiped his nose on the back of his hand. "I figured he'd be out here mucking up somebody's work or snooping around. Yes, I cut the power. I wanted to stop him in his tracks wherever he was."

"And not leave a trace that you were out here," Thibault said.

"He was in Z's cage. I don't remember what happened exactly. I grabbed the stick out of the door handle. I hit him. It made an awful noise. He fell, his head hit the cement." He inhaled with a quivering breath. "I went out, closing the door behind me and knew I had to get rid of the stick. I thought about pitching it somewhere, but I was afraid Victor was around and would see me. I jammed it in my pocket, ran down to the other wing, got a key stick from there and put it outside Z's cage. I figured with all the commotion the next day maybe no one would catch on. Besides, several people have master keys. I drove like hell out of here and chucked the key out the window near the entrance to the road."

Thank you for that, Thibault thought.

"And then you went back to his apartment and erased the files."

Ty began sobbing more loudly and held his hand out to Paige. She moved away slightly, with her hands crossed over her purse.

"I don't know anything about any of this. I wasn't with him out here that night," she said to Thibault. "I had no idea he was capable of such a thing."

Thibault regarded her cool stare and detachment and was surprised to feel sorry for Ty. He took his arm and raised him up. "Come on," he said as he turned him toward the door.

There was a stampeding sound of footsteps on the stairs,

and they all stood still while Henry Simmons came running up to the Werners' office.

"I saw it! I saw it!" he yelled and laughed at the same time. "Z's having her baby!"

He ran back out and the Werners, Paige and Bettina followed him quickly, leaving Victor Allen fumbling with his cane in an attempt to catch up. It only left Thibault in the room with Ty and Gemma.

"Don't think about it," Thibault warned, taking handcuffs from his pocket and reading him his Miranda rights.

"How could you possibly know where I threw that stick?" Ty asked.

"I didn't until you just told me." He took him by the elbow and led him toward the exit.

Chapter 23

The storm had begun in earnest that evening and raged on until morning. Thibault had been up most of the night getting Ty's statement and processing him. After a few hours' sleep, he stood on the porch admiring the spectacular, clear day in progress and wondered if Gemma was standing by the window in her apartment, looking out, thinking of him. Or was she sleeping in after an exhausting day? He wanted to call her but thought she must be as exhausted as he was.

After breakfast, he walked down the path leading from the house to the pines at the eastern portion of his property and began enthusiastically chopping the huge limbs that had been felled by the storm. No chain saw for him; he wanted to exhaust himself physically today after the long hours and lack of exercise last week. Besides, he had to go into work in the afternoon and begin another round of paperwork and discussions with the prosecutor's office. Right now, it felt good to be out in the relatively cool air and dappled shade swinging an axe. He had abandoned his tee shirt early in the enterprise and now was sweating profusely in the humidity, rivulets following the creases of his torso.

As he worked, he thought about a house project for the coming year. He usually liked to save thinking about such things for those long, quiet hours fishing, but he thought he would indulge himself today. Many times he had thought about putting a fireplace in his bedroom, but everybody had talked him out of it. Too expensive, buy a freestanding stove. But it wasn't what he wanted. He wasn't looking for a way to keep the room warm; the whole second story stayed fairly warm in the winter, even with the thermostat low downstairs. He didn't want heat necessarily; he wanted a fireplace. He liked the thought of lying on the bed, listening to the snapping and crackling of the wood. Now, the incredible number of fallen branches from the storm would give him enough wood for the downstairs fireplace for most of the winter and enough chopping work for many weekends ahead. He paused to catch his breath and wipe the sweat off his face and chest with the tee shirt and resumed chopping.

Thibault figured he might be done with the Walter Benson business by the end of the coming week, so he might be able to take his vacation after that. His brother couldn't go with him this year because of some work schedule change, so he would be going all by himself. That was okay. He turned his attention to the garden project and what he should plan to plant for the next year. He stopped again to wipe off his face and heaving chest.

"Hey," said a voice behind him.

Thibault turned and saw Gemma smiling at him.

"Hey, yourself," he said, still breathing heavily. He put his shirt down. "I was just thinking about you," he said honestly. For all of the thoughts of a fireplace, planting a garden, even fishing, had included her presence.

"While frantically chopping wood? That's doesn't sound good." She walked closer. "I'm sorry to startle you, but I guess you couldn't hear the car drive up way out here. I knocked on the door and walked all around before I heard the sound of the axe."

"Well, at least you seem to have wheels now."

"Loaner," she said. "The mechanic was pretty mortified at the continuing failures. We'll see what he manages to find wrong and hopefully fix this next time."

Thibault wanted to say something, anything, everything, but also didn't feel like talking. He thought if he said something, it would all come to an end sooner.

Gemma turned and looked for a dry place to sit, but most of the logs were still soaked. "Do you have a few minutes?"

"Come on, let's go up to the house. I'm parched."

They walked slowly, Thibault mopping his face and neck with his shirt.

"I'm having a hard time with all this," she said.

He nodded but did not say anything. They didn't speak again until they sat side by side on his porch in the sunlight, looking out over the ragged field. A bird trilled from the top of a weedy stalk.

"Mockingbird, right?"

He laughed. "Sorry, meadowlark, but good try."

She laughed, too. "I went into the Colter Center this morning to get my things and Victor Allen was there. With a cane. Seems he bruised his hip when he fell chasing an intruder the other night."

"Aha! The mystery stalker."

"Yeah, oops." She giggled a bit. "Klaus was there, too. He apologized to me. And I apologized to him."

"Well, Kumbaya. That's good."

"Paige was there, packing things up as if nothing happened. Amazing!"

"Yes, she's a cool customer, that one," Thibault agreed.

"It's unbelievable," she said shaking her head. Her hair swung across her face, and he caught the scent of jasmine.

"She just wants everyone to know she had nothing to do with it, I suppose."

"Do you think that's true?" Gemma asked.

He shrugged. "Probably. Dunno."

She picked up a small stick and poked at the step near her foot. "In another month she'll be in California, the land of new beginnings. All this sordid stuff behind her. God, how do you deal with people like that every day?"

"It's not every day. But it's the job. You get used to it." He brushed the burrs off the bottoms of his blue jeans.

"I'm having a hard time with this," she said again. This time he knew she was talking about him.

Thibault looked out at the field in front of them.

"You tend to shut down a bit when you work, don't you?" She looked at him.

"A bit. Not as much as most."

"Oh, I know, it's professional and all that. But you can switch on and off, just like how you switch your language. Like you've had a lot of practice not showing emotion."

He didn't have an answer to that. There was a lot he wanted to say but didn't know where to begin, so they sat in silence for a bit.

"Klaus has offered to put up the money for Ty's lawyer, you know," she said.

"After all his bluster? He's really something. Well, there's a public defender ready to come in if he doesn't follow through." He shook his head in wonder.

"He un-fired me, too. Or, I guess I un-quit. Whichever." She smiled at him. "But I've asked for a week off just to get my thoughts together. After I get the blasted newsletter out and deal with the media inquiries in the next few days."

He waited what seemed like a long moment. "How would you like to go fishing?"

She turned to look into his eyes, her brows coming together slightly. A smile curled the corner of her mouth. "Do you think it could work?"

"Might could," he answered.

～

Reviews help readers discover my books, so feel free to leave a short line or two on my

REVIEW PAGE

THANK YOU!

～

Read the next in the Series:
MURDER IN THE COASTAL DUNES
Gemma is looking forward to time off from her new job while Thibault is grumbling about his. A vacation is the answer, but a stay at the coast turns into an investigation of a death of a museum docent, disappearing artifacts and a drug deal in the making.

～

Do you like historical cozy mysteries? You'll love the
BERKSHIRES COZY SERIES
MURDER AT HIGHFIELDS
Or the **MASSACHUSETTS COZY MYSTERIES.**
Link to Murder on Boston Common
MURDER ON BOSTON COMMON
For more updates, check out my newsletter:
www.Andreas-books.com

Printed in Great Britain
by Amazon

55698640R00145